PRAISE FOR
Lizzy and the
Good Luck Girl

"Readers are in luck! *Lizzy and the Good Luck Girl* is a lively tale of compassion and self-discovery, with a perfect blend of humor, heart, and hope. Lizzy's optimism, drive, and quirky belief in signs from the universe make her a character worth rooting for."

—**Anna Staniszewski, author of *The Dirt Diary***

"Lizzy's desperate need for luck tugged at my heart. Bittersweet, beautiful, and recommended for anyone who's searched for a sign that things will turn out okay—or worried that they might not."

—**Kelly Jones, author of *Unusual Chickens for the Exceptional Poultry Farmer***

"Brimming with small-town charm, quirky characters, and clever humor, *Lizzy and the Good Luck Girl* showcases just how courageous we must be to hold on to hope, especially after loss."

—**Beth Vrabel, author of *The Reckless Club, Caleb and Kit,* and the Pack of Dorks series**

"Readers will root for the memorable, kindhearted protagonist in this engaging story about loss and recovery."

—**Martha Freeman, author of *Zap!* and the Secret Cookie Club series**

"Lizzy Sherman is the kind of kid you want to give a hug and a high-five to, as she tries to make the world a better place one lost cat (and one runaway kid!) at a time. I feel very fortunate to have found Susan Lubner's fresh, funny, and utterly unforgettable novel, *Lizzy and the Good Luck Girl,* which winningly imparts the wisdom that it's not enough to just hold on to lucky things . . . sometimes, you also need to let go."

—**Erica S. Perl, author of *All Three Stooges* and *When Life Gives You O.J.***

LIZZY AND THE GOOD LUCK GIRL

Susan Lubner

RP | KIDS
PHILADELPHIA

Running Press Kids
Hachette Book Group
1290 Avenue of the Americas, New York, NY 10104
www.runningpress.com/rpkids
@RP_Kids

Printed in the United States of America

First Edition: November 2018

Published by Running Press Kids, an imprint of Perseus Books, LLC, a subsidiary of Hachette Book Group, Inc. The Running Press Kids name and logo is a trademark of the Hachette Book Group.

The Hachette Speakers Bureau provides a wide range of authors for speaking events. To find out more, go to www.hachettespeakersbureau.com or call (866) 376-6591.

The publisher is not responsible for websites (or their content) that are not owned by the publisher.

Print book cover and interior design by Frances J. Soo Ping Chow.
Interior art: GettyImages/Embra

Library of Congress Control Number: 2017959794

ISBNs: 978-0-7624-6502-6 (hardcover), 978-0-7624-6504-0 (ebook)

LSC-C

10 9 8 7 6 5 4 3 2 1

TO NANA RUTH

who's with me always

CHAPTER 1

I'D BROUGHT HOME STRAYS BEFORE. PLENTY OF cats and a one-eyed poodle. But never a human. And not without my parents knowing.

The day started like a regular fall Saturday: dark and cold. November suns always took their sweet time rising. My cat Fudge had woken me once already when it was still pitch-black. Here he was again, marching across my pillow and pulling my hair. At least now it was light outside.

"Are you kidding me?" I asked. "It's a good thing you're cute." I reached over my head and pulled him close, pressing his nose against mine. He purred and dropped his head against my cheek. I kissed his fuzzy striped face. Then he stared at me with his green eyes and tapped me on the chin with a paw.

Below my bedroom, plates clattered, muffled voices shouted

out orders, and every once in a while I could hear the scuff of feet or the scrape of a chair move across the black-and-white checkerboard floor. We live on the west side of East Thumb, Maine, on the corner of Abbott and Greenleaf and right smack on top of our diner, the Thumbs-Up. Dad had long gone downstairs to work. Usually, Mom would have been with him at the diner already, too, and by the time they opened at five thirty, Dad would take charge of the griddle, and she would take charge of pretty much everything else.

"Fill the water glasses before the customers' butts hit the chair," she'd tell the servers. "Cut the potatoes into wedges. They look tastier," she'd tell Dad, even though the little squares cooked faster.

These days, with her belly full of baby again, Mom didn't get to work until close to ten, and she took Saturdays off altogether. She didn't freak about half-empty water glasses or the shape of fried potatoes anymore, either. The baby was due to arrive in seven weeks, and Mom smiled at everything because of it—the rain, the bowl of fruit on the kitchen counter, stupid bumper stickers on cars. I hoped her smiley state of mind was a good sign. That we'd be lucky and all would go well this time with this pregnancy.

Fudge wiggled out of my arms and went back to standing on my hair. Life seemed pretty easy for a cat. All you needed was a half-decent place to sleep and some food. Not like my life, which lately seemed the opposite of easy. Thinking about it, my brain felt snarled and tangled like a sticky ball of spaghetti.

First, I worried about Mom and the baby a lot. A couple of weeks ago, Mom thought she had felt a contraction. It scared the daylights out of all of us that she could have been going into labor way before she was supposed to. Thankfully, it turned out to be a false alarm. But ever since it happened, she'd seemed extra tired and looked kind of pale.

The other thing I couldn't get out of my head was the stray who I'd seen going in and out of the empty apartment house across the street. What if she had kittens? I once read in a book that pregnant cats will seek out shelter. Maybe that's why she liked that apartment? And had she found the small pile of tuna I had left for her yesterday? I guess life wasn't always so easy for cats, after all.

My bed shook when the door to the diner opened and slammed shut. A sign. *Get up! Get going!*

I dressed, brushed my teeth, and then poked my head into my parents' room. Mom snored in her sleep, and I could hear her nose whistle from the doorway.

Our other cat, Reuben, snoozed at the far end of the bed. Waffles, our poodle, had learned the hard way to keep his distance from that cat. He snuggled against Mom in a neat ball. His tail batted against the quilt when he saw me with his one eye.

"Shhhhhh...," I told him, and closed the door gently.

In the kitchen, I pulled a hunk off of last night's chicken and wrapped it in foil. Then I grabbed my coat and bag from the rack, tossed on a scarf, and scrambled outside into the cold sunshine.

The wind pushed me like it had hands. Was it saying *hurry up*?

I never used to wonder what it meant when the wind blew against my back, or if an acorn dropped from a tree and knocked me on the head. I never studied the shape of a cloud and thought that the sky might be trying to tell me something. But since the car accident two years ago, I had started paying attention to everything.

My BFF Joss waved to me from the top of the alley that ran beside the diner. We were both wrapped up to our noses in identical Joss-knitted scarves.

"Hey, Lizzy," she said. "Did you bring food?"

"Of course." I patted the outside of the bag slung across my hip.

"I brought a meatball," she told me.

"She'll love it. What about the cat sweater designs?"

"What about them?" Joss whipped a roll of papers out of her back pocket and waved them around.

Joss and I had come up with an idea to knit and sell sweaters for cats. We were doing it to raise money for the Community Lodge for Cats & Dogs (the fancy name for the East Thumb animal shelter) where we volunteered. Next Saturday, we were having a cat sweater sidewalk sale in front of the diner. Franny, the Lodge director, was helping us out with it. She thought our idea was awesome. But not Phil, who worked with Franny. He said cats were too temperamental to be "keen" on wearing sweaters. And I could tell that Sid from the diner was iffy, too, just by the slow way he had nodded his head and said, "Oh really," when we first told him about it.

"Dogs wear sweaters all the time, why not cats?" I had told all the haters. And our teacher, Ms. Santorelli, not only wanted a sweater for her cat, but she wanted us to talk about our fundraiser to the class on Monday.

We crossed the street. Abbott Avenue was noisy with traffic and dotted with gas stations and convenience stores, but Greenleaf Lane was quiet and lined with fat trees, chain-link fences, and apartment houses.

Sandwiched between two dirt lots, diagonally across from the Thumbs-Up, a three-story apartment house loomed like a mangled shipwreck in front of us. A huge tree, which still had a lot of faded leaves hanging from its branches, crowned the roof as if it were trying to help pretty up the place.

We stopped on the sidewalk in front of the porch. A rusty number 4 dangled off an even rustier mailbox attached to a piece of siding. A couple of long planks of wood had been nailed across the door. KEEP OUT was painted on one of the planks in orange paint. If paint could talk, those two words would be screaming at us.

"The last time I saw the cat, she jumped in there." I pointed to a loose sheet of plastic over a first floor window.

Joss rewrapped her scarf. Even without our matching knit-wear we looked like a pair. Shoulder-length brown hair. Blue eyes. Freckles.

"Come on," she said, grabbing my hand. We hurried up the rickety steps. "The tuna is gone. She must be here."

We moved closer to the broken window. I peeked in.

"Wait," Joss said, taking a step back, "is this like breaking in? I don't want to go to jail or anything."

"It's okay to break the law to save a life. *Lives* if there are kittens, too," I said. "Plus, they don't put twelve-year-olds in jail." Though I wasn't positive about that.

"What makes you so sure the cat has kittens?" Joss asked me.

"Why else would she keep going in there?"

"How about to get out of the cold?"

"Maybe. But if you were a *hungry* cat," I said.

"Which I'm not."

"But if you were, wouldn't you hang out at the back door of a diner instead of here? That's just common sense."

Joss nodded.

The wind grabbed a bunch of dried up leaves that were piled in the corners of the porch and whipped them around our feet. A big fat warning sign? *Trouble is swirling around me*? Or maybe *opportunity at my feet*! Which was it?

Joss watched me watching the leaves. "They're just leaves. Nothing else," she said as if she could read my mind, which I really believed she could sometimes.

"Let's go," I said.

I checked the rotted windowsill for broken glass that might be sticking up, then I pulled back the tattered plastic and stepped through. Joss followed.

"It's not so bad in here compared to how dumpy it is on the outside," I said, looking around.

"I was thinking the same thing. Except for the dead leaves." There were little mounds of them everywhere.

The room we stood in was round. Sun poured through tall windows, and we both squinted. There was a plaid recliner with the stuffing coming out of one arm next to a massive fireplace that took up half of one wall. A mirror hung over the mantel, with a few cracks zigzagged through its glass—a sign of bad luck for someone—though I didn't break it, so not me! A pair of doors with fancy glass knobs opened up into a hallway.

"No cat here," Joss said, checking underneath the chair.

The house turned way darker and a whole lot colder as we

walked down the hallway, away from the sunny round room. There were fewer windows, and most were boarded up or covered in plastic.

In the kitchen, I peeked inside an open cabinet under the sink. One of the doors had fallen off and it looked like a nice hiding spot for a cat. But all I found was a dirty towel and a box of damp matches.

Back in the hall, Joss tapped her cell phone and turned on the flashlight. The floor lit up in front of us, and we stepped inside a bathroom. The tub was full of grime and enough dead leaves to hide under.

"This bath needs a bath," Joss joked.

Above us, something made a loud *snap*. We both jumped.

"What was that?" Joss grabbed my arm.

We heard it again, but this time it was softer. I pointed to the torn plastic over a broken window just above the toilet. "I think the wind must have caught it," I said.

We were back in the hallway heading toward another room when Joss stopped suddenly. I smacked into her.

"What's wrong?" I asked.

"I heard a little squeak."

"Heeeere, kitty, kitty," I sang in a high-pitched voice. I unwrapped the chicken.

We peered inside a bedroom. "Look!" I pointed to a hole at the bottom of a closet door. We walked closer, and the gray cat jumped out at my feet. "Hey, you! There you are!"

"She looks hungry," Joss said, kneeling to pet her. But before Joss or I had a chance to offer it food, the cat scooted back inside the closet.

"See! I bet she has kittens in there!" I opened the door. Joss shined the light inside. Right away I saw the bulging backpack.

Two yellow sneakers that I nearly stepped on.

Two jean-covered knees tucked under a chin.

A small hand with a tiny tattoo.

Joss screamed and dropped her cell phone. I screamed, too. The cat shot out of the room like a rocket.

And the girl in the closet said a single word:

"Impossible."

CHAPTER 2

"WHAT'S IMPOSSIBLE?" I ASKED. MY HEART WAS still pretty revved up and it raced against my chest.

"Kittens," she said.

"Lizzy! Let's go!" Joss pulled at my arm. But I didn't budge. The girl hugged her bag against her body and wiggled backward a bit, trying to press herself closer to the wall inside the closet. Her huge eyes stared up at me, never turning away from mine. If she was afraid, she was trying hard not to show it.

"It's dark in here! Where's my phone?!" Joss bent down and swiped at the floor.

"It's over there." The girl pointed to the left. Joss quickly found it. She tapped the flashlight back on, which seemed to calm her down. Then, she aimed it at the closet. The girl put her hand up to block the light from her eyes.

"Joss! You're blinding her!" I saw that the girl had red hair the color of a penny. It stopped just above her shoulders and she had it tucked behind her ears. Her bangs stuck up in a few places across her forehead. Her face was angled like an upside-down triangle with wide bony cheeks and a pointed chin. It was hard to tell how old she was. Our age? Older?

"Sorry," Joss said to her. "I was just looking for kittens." She turned the light toward a corner, but there was just empty space, no cat or babies.

"Kittens are impossible for that cat. It's a *he*-cat not a *she*-cat," said the girl. She was staring at the chicken I held in my hand.

"Do you want this?" I asked her.

"Can I?" Her voice was soft.

"Want this, too?" Joss offered her the meatball.

The girl took the food and pushed it into her mouth. "Fnanks," she said, chewing. The cat was back. She saved a little piece of the chicken and meatball for him, which he quickly gobbled up.

"So the cat's a he?" I asked.

She nodded.

"We thought the cat had some kittens in here because she was coming in and out of the house," Joss explained.

"*He*," the girl said. She smiled. Her eyes crinkled at the edges, like it was kind of funny that we kept forgetting *she* was a *he*.

"Is this where you live?" I asked her.

11

"Not really. Well, sort of. For now, I guess."

"Why are you here?"

"How come *you're* here?" she asked me back. She tipped her head to the side.

Joss stepped closer to me and whispered, "Maybe we should go."

I shook my head no. "We told you why we're here. We thought there might be kittens in this house."

"Nope. Just me and Smoky."

"Smoky?" I asked.

"The cat. Because he's gray," Joss said. "Smoky gray." He curled himself around my leg as if to say, *Yup! That's me!*

"Do you have anything else to eat?" she asked. "Please."

"I can get you something else," I told her.

"Really?" She hopped up onto her knees and unzipped her backpack, digging inside it for a second. She pulled out a large paper bag. "If I have to be, I'm okay." She peeked into the crumpled sack. "I only brought peanut butter and jelly with me. I've eaten three of the ten sandwiches already. I'm so sick of peanut butter. Oh, and I brought this." She held up a sorry-looking banana covered in brown spots. "And I forgot to pack a drink." She stuck her tongue out. Then she smiled again. But, this time, her eyes weren't smiling. I saw that they looked sad.

"Joss and I have to work at my parents' diner until three

thirty. Then we can bring you something. Can you wait that long?" I checked my cell phone for the time. Almost nine thirty. "Or I could go home and bring you back something now."

"I'll be okay. Do you think you can bring me some more chicken?" she asked. "I love chicken. I mean, whatever would be great. Anything but peanut butter, you know?"

"I can get you chicken," I told her.

"And something to drink. Do you have Coke? Please."

"Sure," I said.

"I never get to drink it at home," she told us. She waved her hand slightly. I saw a flash of the tattoo. It was right above the V between her thumb and index finger. It was green, but that's all I could see that it was.

"What's your name?" I asked her. "I'm Lizzy."

"Joss." Joss waved.

The girl didn't answer. It seemed like she was thinking it might not be a good idea for us to know. Then she said, "I'll tell you after you bring me more food, okay?" She sat back down, pulling her bag onto her lap and hugging it close.

"Okay," said Joss. "We'll be back. Come on, Lizzy. Let's go."

"Hold on," I said. I unwrapped my scarf and dropped it around the girl's neck. "Here. You can keep this. I have another one."

"Good idea," Joss said to me. I was glad she didn't mind, since she had knit it for me.

"Thanks. It's so cold in here," the girl said. It seemed like it took an extra wrap around her neck to get it on right. She was small.

In the shadowy light she reminded me of a rare bird I had seen in a book, with the scarf under her bony face and the way some of the hair across her forehead stood up in little spikes, like it was exasperated.

"You can't tell anyone I'm here," she told us.

The sound of her voice felt like a kick to my stomach. I didn't even know her, but somehow I suddenly wanted to protect her. "We won't," I said.

"I'm serious." The girl rubbed her nose with the back of her hand. She was wearing a coat that didn't seem ratty at all. Someone must have cared enough about her to make sure she had a nice warm jacket. *Or maybe not,* I reconsidered. She had run away, after all.

"We won't say a word. We promise," Joss told her.

Outside, we walked quickly toward the diner. "This is weird," I said. "How long do you think she's been there?"

"For as long as it takes a banana to turn brown?"

"I guess," I said. "How long is that?"

"I don't know. Maybe it was almost brown when she got here. Maybe it's only been a day or two," Joss said.

I hoped so. "I can't picture having to stay in that cold house by myself even for one night."

"Someone must be sad not knowing where she is," Joss said. She kicked a rock and it made a *clink* when it hit the fence.

"Maybe she ran away for a good reason," I said. "Maybe she had to."

"But why?"

"I don't know. I've seen stuff on TV before about parents who hurt their kids." That was harder to think about than living in a dark house and eating only peanut butter and rotting bananas.

Joss stopped walking for a second. "I've seen stuff like that, too," she said. She put her hand across her mouth as if she had just realized something that made her feel scared and uneasy.

I was feeling pretty uneasy myself. A girl hiding in a closet. A cat named Smoky. They had to be signs of something.

I wondered what.

CHAPTER
3

"HEEEEEEEEEY! IT'S LIZZY PANCAKES AND HER matching sidekick!" Sid Valentine carried a tray full of omelets so fat the guts were spilling out. Sid was tall and skinny and as bald as a cue ball, with a beard and a mustache like a pirate. When he zipped by, he popped his fake front tooth out and back in, and Joss and I laughed. Sid did that whenever we asked him to (and sometimes when we didn't). But he always made sure no customers were looking, and he used his tongue not his hands, so no germs were involved.

"You should get a gold tooth," Joss told him once. But Sid was way too nice to be a pirate, anyway.

The Thumbs-Up was always crowded. Joss and I waited by the door for two stools to free up at the counter. The counter ran parallel to the kitchen, down one side of the diner. On the other side, four booths with shiny red seats took up the entire wall. In between were eight tables, most with two or four chairs, except for the one where a couple of the tables had been pushed together to accommodate a bigger party.

Most of the Thumbs-Up's walls were covered in old Coke and Pepsi signs my mom and dad had collected from flea markets, plus a colorful metal sign mounted over the kitchen that read: EAT HERE, THE FOOD IS GOOD. And hanging from the ceiling, in the center of everything, was the front half of an old Chevy, because a whole car was too big to fit. It was black with white wheels to match our checkerboard floor.

Joss and I waved to Cooper and Zoe, friends from school, who were at a table with Cooper's parents.

I looked beyond the counter and the half wall into the kitchen. Through the open space I saw Dad sweating over the griddle. To the left of that opening, a blackboard hung where yours truly posted all of the specials. Not only was I a whiz at sandwich naming, but I had really neat handwriting, too.

"Order up!" Dad hollered. He slid a plate piled with scrambled eggs and steaming home fries onto the shiny metal countertop in front of him and stuck an order slip underneath.

"Good morning, lovelies!" Bibi hollered to us over two towers of french toast. She hustled to deliver the stacked plates, her dark ponytail swinging back and forth behind her shoulders.

Bibi liked to wear funky-looking sneakers she called *practical with pizazz*. Today's pair was covered in leopard spots. Another pair had lemons and limes. She sometimes wore a pair that looked like they had graffiti all over them. But her favorites were the black-and-white checkered sneakers because she got a kick out of matching the diner floor.

She snatched up some menus and scooted over to greet the two policemen who had come in behind us.

"Welcome to the Thumbs-Up diner!" Bibi said to them, like they'd never been in before. That's how she greeted all the customers, regulars and "newbies." The whole of the East Thumb police force, all two of them, came in for a danish and coffee about three times a day.

The officers followed Bibi to a table. Each kept a hand on his belt right by his gun, probably ready to shoot, just in case something bad happened. It crossed my mind that maybe they secretly wished something bad would happen, because nothing police-worthy ever happened in East Thumb. Mostly, the cops seemed bored out of their skulls. I'd bet they'd want to know about a girl hiding out in the apartment house across the street.

A couple of stools finally opened up, and Joss and I plopped onto them. Joss pulled out her sweater sketches and unrolled them.

Dad looked up from the griddle. "Hey there," he said. "What's happening?"

Oh, not much. We just found a hungry girl hiding in a closet, that's all. Instead, I told him, "Fudge woke me up again. Twice!"

Dad threw his hands in the air, still clutching a spatula in one. "That Fudge!" He pretended to be angry. "To boldly go where no cat has gone before!" he said, shaking his head. Joss laughed.

"Dad!" I was not a Star Trek fan. Dad swore he was no Trekker or Trekkie (there was a difference, apparently), but he liked to quote old Star Trek TV shows and movies. Sometimes he replaced a word from an original line with one of his own that he thought made it funny. Like calling his pickup truck "the East Thumb Enterprise," after the Star Trek spaceship.

"How's the cat sweater business?" Sid asked, scooting behind the counter. He poured us water and set down silverware wrapped in a napkin. "Ready for your big event next Saturday?"

"We will be," I told him.

"I've never heard of a cat wearing a sweater." He wiped down the area in front of us while carefully avoiding Joss's sketches.

"That's why it's such a brilliant idea. What word did your mom call it?" I asked Joss.

"Novel."

"Right," I said. "It's that."

"You've got to be pretty brave to dress a cat," he said before walking away.

"Hey," I said to Joss, "we should have some of the shelter cats and kittens at our event. Maybe some of them could get adopted right on the spot."

Joss nodded. She was watching the little TV that was mounted from the ceiling in front of us. "That's the girl! On the news!" she whispered at me, her eyes still focused on the screen. "Look!"

I looked up at the screen just as a commercial came on.

"Where?" I asked.

"It was the girl in the closet! You missed it."

"Are you sure? What's her name? Where'd she come from?"

"I didn't hear. I only saw it for a few seconds, but it was the girl's face taking up the whole screen."

"Someone is looking for her!" My heart was skipping. I glanced behind me at Officer Hodge and Sergeant Blumstein, as if by looking at them I could gauge if they were starting to suspect that I was hiding something. I hoped I didn't look as guilty as I suddenly felt.

"What are we supposed to do?" I asked.

"Nothing," Joss said. "We promised her we wouldn't say anything, remember?"

We had promised, but it felt awful knowing something that someone else might be desperate to know, too.

"Maybe if we tell the girl she was on the news, she'll go home," Joss continued.

"Maybe." I had no idea if she would or wouldn't, but Joss just saying that she might made me feel better. "Let's talk cat sweaters, instead," I said.

Joss poked her finger at the first little drawing. Not only could she knit super well, but her sketches were great. "I know lots of dog sweaters have sleeves, but I'm just going with leg holes. Cats aren't as patient as dogs, so I'm keeping it simple," she said.

I nodded. We knew our sweaters wouldn't be for every cat, like Joss's cat Marco and my Reuben, who were grumps. But lots of cats, like Fudge, who I had dressed in socks and T-shirts before, were totally easygoing.

"Then there's this." She unrolled a second sketch to show me a sweater with pockets on the back.

"Why pockets?" I asked.

"To hold cat treats."

"A cat with a treat stuffed inside a pocket could attract a wild animal. Or a dog. It's kind of like bait."

"Hmmm . . ." Joss pressed her hand against her face. "True. We'll skip the pocket option."

"Like you said, keep it simple," I told her.

I pulled my notebook out of the bag that was still slung across my hip. "I thought up three names for our sweaters. Which one do you like best? CatKnits? Get it? Like catnip . . . but *CatKnit*?" Joss shook her head, which I didn't mind because it wasn't my favorite, either. "How about Knitty Kitty?"

"Cozy Cat!" she shouted, pointing to the third choice. "I love it!"

"Yup, me too." I made a little check mark next to it. Then Joss and I fist-bumped. I had just closed my notebook when Sid fake-tossed my plate of pancakes, flicking his wrist like he was about to throw a Frisbee to me. I flinched.

"Fake out!" he hollered and waited for us to move our stuff. He served Joss her fried eggs and placed my plate gently in front of me. Some of the blueberries had burst, and the stack was soaked with little pools of dark purple.

"Yum. Thanks, Sid." I reached for my water. The ice cubes inside the glass swirled and formed a smiley face. My heart blew up like a puffer fish. A random happy face was always a good sign. How could it not be? As soon as I thought that, the ice shifted and the smile was gone. *Happiness is short-lived.* The thought paralyzed me for a split second.

"I'm saving this for the girl in the closet," Joss said quietly a few minutes later. She had finished her breakfast except for the bacon, which she wrapped in her napkin and tucked inside her coat pocket.

Bibi whizzed by us with an armload of dirty dishes. "Chop, chop, girls! I could really use your help bussing tables," she said.

Joss took our coats and my bag to hang up in the back while I quickly finished eating, still wondering about those ice cubes in my glass and the trickiness of signs. What were the ice cubes trying to tell me?

Some signs were obvious. Like a street sign, that straight-out told you that you were standing on the corner of Abbott and Greenleaf. The other kind of sign, like the ice cube kind, well, they only told you that you were standing on the corner of *something*. It was up to you to figure out what that something was.

. One thing I had learned to be true is that the not-so-obvious signs were everywhere if you paid close attention—even in the shape of a puffy cloud or in the song of a bird outside your window. Sometimes they appeared out of nowhere. Like on the hand of a total stranger. In the shape of a tiny tattoo. A sign that might be super important, if it were actually meant for you.

CHAPTER 4

AT THREE O'CLOCK, SID WAS STIRRING THE STOCK
for tomorrow's soup.

The last two customers paid their bill. Dad waved to them as
they walked out the door. "Have a good one!" he said. He flipped
the orange sign in the window to CLOSED. Then he moved behind
the half wall to clean the griddle. His sloped belly bumped up
against the edge with each forward scrub.

I heard the metal click of the time clock from the back room,
Bibi clocking out.

"I have to say, I am proud of you girls," she said to Joss and me
before leaving. "I've always said it's a nice thing to stick your hand
out when someone needs it. I hope those furry little sugar packets appreciate all you're doing for that shelter. See you two sugar
cookies soon," she said to us. Her sneakers made a squeaky sound

as she strolled toward the door.

Joss refilled salt shakers and collected the ketchup bottles from the tables.

"What's the soup tomorrow?" I asked Sid, erasing the old specials off the blackboard.

"Chicken vegetable," he said.

"We've got to go," Joss was whispering in my ear. "Let's get her food."

"I'm almost ready," I said. I dropped the chalk into the little metal tray, leaving a blank space on the board. I got paid a little extra to come up with the sandwich special of the "every other day or so." But I hadn't thought of a new one yet.

Dad came around the counter holding a mug and a large bottle of the colored tablets he was always chewing to help with his heartburn. Mom liked to tease Dad a little bit about it because his stomach problems started when she got pregnant. She joked that she was the one who was supposed to have the heartburn, not him, since it was a common thing for a pregnant woman.

"We're hungry," I told Dad.

"Grab a sandwich," he said, taking a seat behind a stack of papers and mail.

In the back kitchen, I pulled a plastic container out of the refrigerator. "What's in here?" I asked, lifting the top off.

"Chicken! Just what the girl ordered," Joss said to me.

"Ah! Not that. That's for the soup." We hadn't noticed that Sid had followed us in. He reached around me and pulled it out of my hands.

"How about just a tiny piece?" Joss asked.

"How about chicken salad? I made a fresh batch of that." He slid the container back in the fridge.

"Chicken salad will work," Joss said.

"Yeah. It's still chicken," I said.

"Still chicken," Sid said, looking a little bit confused. "You want your sandwiches on a roll or wrap?"

"Roll," we both answered.

"Can we have an extra sandwich to split?" I asked.

"Really?"

"We are soooooo hungry," I said, slumping my shoulders and hanging my arms toward the ground like I was weak and tired.

"Yeah," Joss said, copying my exaggerated slump. "We worked our butts off."

"You sure did. Three sandwiches coming up."

"Oh, and can you make them to go?" I asked. "Please," I added.

"Yes, ma'am."

While Sid went back out front to make the sandwiches, Joss and I snuck into the giant fridge. I wrapped up a few slices of salami and some roast beef and dropped them into my bag. I added a hunk of cheddar cheese, a fresh banana, and some packets of the oyster crackers we served with the chowder and soups.

We grabbed our coats. Then I filled an extra-large cup with ice and Coke. "All this food will make her thirstier than she probably already is."

Dad was still at the counter doing paperwork. He swiped his hand over the top of his no-fair-hair, as Mom and Sid liked to call it. Sid, because his own hair had started thinning when he and Dad were just seniors in high school together almost twenty years ago, and Mom, because it was thicker and shinier than her own and Dad could not have cared less about it. "Perfect hair, wasted on the wrong person," she'd joke.

"Order up!" Sid handed us the three sandwiches each wrapped in white paper with a smiling cat face he had drawn.

"Cute!" I said to him. "Thanks."

"I'm a man of many talents," he told us, pushing his tooth out and in. Joss and I laughed.

"See ya," I called out to Dad.

Joss held her hand out toward my father, pressing her pointer and middle finger together and her ring and pinky together, leaving a large *V* in the middle. The Vulcan salute. Dad saluted back. I tried, but I couldn't separate my fingers like that unless my ring finger and pinky were bent way forward.

"You have to work on it," he said to me with a wink. Then he swallowed a burp, tossed a couple of those colored pills into his mouth, and chewed quickly. "Why don't you eat here? I'll be working for a while." It was three thirty, and we had told the girl we'd be back by then.

"We have stuff to do," I said.

"What kind of stuff?"

"*Stuff* stuff," I told him.

All of a sudden Dad stood up out of his seat and jerked his head toward the kitchen. "Do you smell that?" he asked us.

"What?" I said.

"Smoke. You two didn't turn anything on back there, did you? The oven? The griddle can't be on, I just finished cleaning it." He sniffed in deeply. "It smells . . . smoky . . ."

Smoky!

I whispered to Joss, "Like the cat!" *A sign.*

Joss tipped her head a bit and raised her eyebrows. It was a look that asked, *Seriously?* and *Are you nuts?* at the same time.

Sid stopped restocking the straws at the counter and double-checked the griddle. "Everything's off. But I smell it, too."

"Me too," Joss said.

"Where's it coming from?" Dad said more to himself than to us. He sprinted to the back room. I heard the back door swing open, Dad's footsteps pounding up the staircase to our apartment, and then the sound of his feet running over my head. I looked up at the diner ceiling.

"Oh no!" I screeched, and ran out after him with Joss and Sid behind me. The back door to our apartment was just a few feet from the back door of the diner and it was wide open. I started up the staircase when Dad came jogging back down.

"It's not coming from our apartment." He exhaled loudly as we followed him back inside the Thumbs-Up.

"I bet it's somebody burning leaves nearby," Sid said.

"Yup. I think you must be right. Though it's too windy a day to be doing that." Dad went back to his work at the counter.

"Let's go," Joss said.

Out the window of the front door, in a small slice of sunlight, I saw tiny flakes of snow swirling. The flakes turned randomly, spinning into a crazy dance. "Hey! Sunshine and snow at the same time!" I said. A sure sign of something weird.

"What the . . . ?" My dad's voice boomed behind me.

"What's going on?" Sid looked up at the ceiling.

I saw it, too.

The orange glow. Like a sunset sinking between the walls of the diner. But the sun wasn't setting.

Outside, the snow fell heavier now. It fluttered like confetti in the street. Except, it wasn't snow.

I yanked open the front door. The string of hanging bells rattled against the wood.

"Holy macaroni," Dad said over my shoulder. Giant orange

flames poked through the top floor windows. Black smoke poured through a hole in the roof. The triple-story apartment house was burning to the ground.

CHAPTER
5

DAD PUNCHED 9-1-1 INTO HIS CELL PHONE BUT hung up fast. Someone had already called for help. Sirens pierced the smoky air and my heart at the same time. Sirens did that to me ever since the accident.

Joss's face looked like someone had just jumped out of the dark and scared her. My own face probably had the same petrified look. I bolted outside and into the road.

"Elizabeth Sherman!" my father shouted behind me. I made it halfway across the street before he grabbed the back of my jacket. "What on earth . . . ?" he said. I looked back at him, my coat all twisted in his grip.

"Dad! Let go!"

"Where do you think you're going?" he asked me.

"LET GO! I need to see!"

"You don't run *toward* a fire! You can see from here!" He pulled me back to the diner where Joss stood outside, her mouth open like it was hanging on a broken hinge.

"I need to GO!" I tried pulling free. My knees shook so badly I thought I might fall down. "DAD, LET GO . . . there's a . . ."

"What's with you, Lizzy?" my dad asked. He tipped his head like he was confused. "You can watch from a safe distance," he said.

Joss suddenly poked me with her elbow. She pointed with her chin, which was back in the right place on her face again. On the other end of the street, the girl, her hood up and most of her face covered with my scarf, stood holding the gray cat and watching the apartment house burn. The sight of her made my knees buckle from relief. I slumped against my dad's thick shoulder.

"Are you okay?" he asked. He put his arm around me.

"I . . . I thought . . . the cat, you know the stray cat?" I asked him. He still looked confused. "I had seen the cat near the house. But I just saw that he's safe."

"Ah. Good," he said. "Can you believe this?"

I shook my head no, but he wasn't talking to me anymore. My mother had come downstairs from our apartment. She walked toward us in her black cowboy boots, wrapped in the wool blanket from the couch, which barely stretched across her big baby belly.

Her blond hair was darker at the top since she stopped

coloring it. It hung just below her shoulders and framed her jaw and neck with a few blunt layers. Her face glowed, partly because of the lights from the trucks. But her skin always had that dewy look to it, even before the pregnancy.

"How did the fire start?" my mother asked calmly. The old Mom would have been freaking out—positive it would spread across the street.

"No idea," Dad said.

"I'll be a son of a gun," Sid said, slowly shaking his head.

My mother rubbed her belly calmly with both hands as if she were telling the baby not to worry. *Everything is okay. You're safe with Momma.*

"We saw the fire when it first happened," I explained. "We were inside the diner and the room turned orange."

"My goodness," my mother said. "It turned orange in the apartment, too."

Smoke spread out from the burning house like a giant black cape. More smoke spewed out and up from the top, as if the building had become one giant chimney. A special for the board popped into my head. The Smoke Stack. A triple-storied sandwich. Smoked salmon, cream cheese, black olives, onion, and tomato layered on three slices of bread instead of two. I felt a twinge guilty that I thought of it at a time like this. So I tucked it away in my brain for later.

Fire trucks arrived, their loud brakes shrieking to a quick stop. An ambulance pulled up, and two women in uniform jumped out. I could hear only bits and pieces of conversations. "Over there! . . . Stand back! . . . Got it!"

Sergeant Blumstein and Officer Hodge showed up.

The whole scene was part scary-cool and part something else. I didn't know what, but it made me feel a little sick.

"It's sad," my mother said. "It's just a house, but it's still a loss."

Yes, I thought, *that was the something else.*

Like the sirens, the red lights brought me back to the night of the car accident, and I felt my throat close. I think they made Mom feel the same way. Because, for just a second, I saw that her dark brown eyes looked even darker. Maybe it was that the daylight was fading, but they definitely had that same blank look they had had back during that awful time. My heart coiled up like a spring, and I looked away from her.

"What should we do about the girl?" Joss asked quietly. She had moved so close I could feel a warm patch on my neck from her breathing.

The girl was still standing in the same spot, holding the cat. She was half turned away from the diner, not looking our way. I stared at the side of her face, willing her to look at me. I wished I could signal that we had food for her.

"She's ignoring us on purpose," I whispered back. I figured she was afraid that if we talked to her, someone, Sid or my parents, who were standing just a few feet behind us, would start asking questions. *Who is that? Introduce us to your friend, Lizzy!*

I jostled the Coke still in my hand. I could tell by the sloshing sound that the ice had started to melt even in the cold air.

"How are we going to get the food to her?" Joss asked me.

"I don't know, but do you think she accidently started the fire?" I whispered.

"I was wondering that, too."

"Maybe she was cold and tried to light something in the fire-place," I said.

The wind blew a strong gust of smoke toward us. Sid coughed. My mom waved her hand in front of her face. "I'm going back inside. Come in, girls," she said as she started walking toward the apartment. "This can't be healthy."

"Yes," Dad said to us, "go on upstairs."

"I should go home," Joss said. I knew her super wide-eyed stare at me was her way of trying to tell me she had an idea. And I knew what it was. She'd leave and get the food to the girl. Except the food was in my bag. And how would I hand all that extra stuff to Joss in front of my dad without it seeming totally weird?

"I'll walk with you," I said.

"No, girls, you won't," my father said. "It's getting dark now. And colder."

I gave Joss a super wide-eyed stare back. *What do we do now?* Joss and I walked to each other's houses all the time. She was just a few blocks away. But neither of us was allowed to walk anywhere in the dark.

"I think the street is blocked up there," Joss said, pointing. She gave me a little smile. I could tell she had an idea, but I didn't understand what she was planning to do.

Two news crews had arrived. There were reporters and cameras. Abbott Avenue was completely jammed and blocked off at both ends. "Joss, stay for dinner. I'll drive you home later," Dad said.

"It's okay. I just texted my mom. She texted back that my sister's coming to pick me up."

Joss's cell phone lit up with another text. "She's going to wait for me up on the corner of Juniper and Greenleaf because the road is closed. I can walk the block by myself." Joss's eyes went wide again.

"I'll walk her to the car," I said, picking up on the plan.

"I'll go with you both. I don't want you walking around in the dark."

"Dad, seriously? It's a block, and there's police and firemen everywhere!"

"All right, all right," Dad said. "I'll grab some steak tips for dinner and close up. You meet me right back here at the diner. It shouldn't take you more than a few minutes to scoot to Juniper, so don't make me worry."

I hooked my arm through Joss's, and we rushed into the crowd. I checked to see if Dad was still watching. I hoped not, because we were heading in the wrong direction, toward where we last saw the girl standing with the cat.

"I don't see her! Where is she?" Joss said at the same time I realized I couldn't see the girl anymore, either. There were so many people. I lifted my head, but I was too short and the street was too jam-packed.

"Keep looking," I said. A bright flash of light hit me in the face. It was someone with a camera from one of the news stations. "Maybe she's gone," I shouted over the noise. "I bet she was scared she'd get on TV by mistake."

Joss slapped her hands against her face. "You're right. I didn't think of that. I'm sure she doesn't have a clue that she's already been on the news."

"No kidding," I said. "I feel bad. She'll be hungry and she's already thirsty. We should have brought her something before we went to work." My eyes darted everywhere, hoping to see her behind a tree, a house, a truck. She was nowhere. "Where would she go?"

"If she started that fire, probably as far away as possible," Joss said.

"You know, if anyone saw us going in and out of that window today, they could blame us for doing something that might have started it."

"No! We were in there way before," Joss said.

"True."

Joss's phone lit up again. A text from her sister. She held it out for me to read.

Move ur butt I'm not ur chauffer!!!!

"Come on. We better go," I said. We turned around and headed to Juniper. Right away we could see Elle's car parked a block ahead.

"See you tomorrow. Don't forget, Elle is going to Portland and she said we could ride in with her to get some yarn."

"It's a plan," I said. Joss ran toward Elle's car, and I headed home.

Dad had already shut off the diner lights and was locking the door. A crowd still clogged the street. The apartment house smoldered. Even though the big flames had been put out, the firemen still had their hoses aimed at it. By now, it was five o'clock and dark, and the bright lights from all the trucks gave everything around me—the pavement, the buildings, the faces on all the people—an eerie shine.

"Good. You're back," Dad said. "Let's get home. I'm pooped." At the bottom of the alley, as soon as we turned into the back parking lot, I saw the gray cat. He was just sitting there, like he was waiting for me.

"Hey!" I said. "Here's the cat!" He jumped up on the hood of my father's truck. "You're a little monkey, aren't you?" I looked around. Was the girl hiding out nearby?

"Who do we have here? The little fella that had you all worried? He's trying to get aboard the East Thumb Enterprise," Dad said. The cat lowered himself into a long stretch, reaching his paws out in front of him, dropping his chest, and arching his bony back. "Don't scratch the paint." We both laughed because Dad's old truck already had a whole bunch of scratches and dings.

The cat jumped down and rubbed up against my legs. "He's so skinny," I said. "I need to bring him in, Dad."

My father knelt down and rubbed the cat's head. "Well, he's already used up one of his lives escaping that fire, right? Let's bring him in. One more furry mouth to feed won't make or break us, I suppose."

I dropped my bag by the door and placed the Coke next to it. I scooped the cat up, tucking him under my chin. I could feel his ribs and his bumpy spine as I ran my hand down his back. I hoped the girl wouldn't mind I was taking him with me. He was hungry, too.

"Where'd the girl go?" I whispered in Smoky's ear.

Then I followed my father inside, leaving my bag and the drink behind.

CHAPTER 6

"HENRY!" THE BANGLED BRACELETS STACKED ON my mother's wrists jangled when she lifted the bowl of potato chips away from Dad. He had a mountain of them piled up on his plate.

Dad laughed. "Aww, come on. I like a little crunch with my meals."

"Chips are not helping solve your heartburn problems. Besides, broccoli is crunchy," she said, biting into a piece.

"Yeah, Dad. Why do you eat chips with everything?" I shoveled a fork full of my mother's squash lasagna into my mouth.

"Why not?" he asked. "Life is short."

"It's probably shorter, *hopefully not,* when you eat like you do," my mother said. "I wish you'd try yoga and a few green vegetables." She closed her eyes for a second and exhaled.

"Forget about yoga. I can barely pick up a dropped spoon. And green vegetables give me gas. It's better for everyone if I avoid them," he said. "You girls, stick with your healthy eating. I like my steak and potato chips."

"I like steak sometimes, too," my mother pointed out. "But you can still ease up on the junk food."

"I'd rather still eat potato chips," Dad said, crunching.

The red lights from the fire trucks flashed inside the apartment as if there was a disco ball hanging from the ceiling. The atmosphere looked like it was calling for a party, but it felt like a bad memory. I wished it would stop.

"When will they shut those darn lights off?" Mom said as if reading my mind. I couldn't tell if she was just annoyed by all of the flashing or if it was something more than that, like it was for me.

Dad dropped little bits of steak onto the floor. "Here's a treat, everyone," he said. Waffles bounced over to the table, and Fudge and Reuben scrambled over for their share.

Reuben hissed at Waffles. Reuben and Fudge may have looked alike with their brown stripy fur and white paws, but Fudge didn't have a cranky or skittish bone in his body. And he wasn't bothered by anything, even a dog five times his size. "Fudge is a simpleton," Dad liked to say. "Not much going on in that cat's head, but it serves him well."

"You're teaching them all how to beg," Mom said.

"They're already experts," I said.

Reuben hissed at Smoky, too, who had been on the opposite side of the kitchen but was carefully coming over to see what Dad was offering. My parents thought Smoky was a perfect name, and I felt a little guilty taking credit for it.

"Be nice to him, Reuben," I warned, in a gentle voice.

"He'll come around," Mom said. "Remember how long it took him to get used to Waffles?"

When Waffles showed up four years ago, besides only having one eye, his black, curly coat was mangy and full of fleas. We found him sniffing for scraps by the Dumpster. Dad said he actually found us because he knew we wouldn't turn him away. Mom said it was because Waffles smelled bacon coming from the diner. But it was love at first sight for all of us.

Waffles was a giant poodle, so he could easily rest his chin on the top of the table, which he was doing right now, next to Dad's elbow.

"That's not very good manners," Mom said to Waffles.

"Awwww . . . you're just a precocious poodle, aren't you?" Dad fed him a potato chip. "He loves them. Like his papa."

"Speaking of potato chips, I was thinking we should add some healthier options to the menu at the diner. All this greasy food isn't good for anybody," Mom said. She leaned into me. "Don't tell anyone else that." She smiled. "Bad for business."

"And highly illogical," my father said in his Mr. Spock voice. "People around here like our food, and if it ain't broke, why fix it?"

"I know they like our food, but we could serve some organic stuff, Henry. People are into that," Mom said.

"Expensive. I'd pay almost double for those fancy eggs."

"You could charge more," I said. Since I was handling the money stuff for Cozy Cat sweaters I felt qualified to point that out.

"Low prices are part of our draw, and if I changed the prices and added items, I'd have to print up new menus. Ka-*ching*!"

Ka-ching was supposed to be the sound of money flying out of Dad's cash register.

"Well, maybe we can revisit this when I'm back to working full-time. After the baby . . ." Mom said, and then stopped. As if just talking about the baby coming might jinx everything.

Babies didn't come easily for Mom and Dad. After me, it had taken so many years for them to finally almost have another. And then the car accident happened, and that baby didn't make it, either.

"Maybe," Mom continued, "we'll add whole wheat pancakes. It doesn't cost much to stock whole wheat flour, does it?"

Dad reached for Mom's hand and squeezed it. "Maybe not."

● ● ●

After dinner, my parents cleared the table and I rinsed the dishes and put them in the dishwasher. The window above the sink overlooked the back parking lot. We kept a couple of lights on out there that gave me a good view of Dad's truck and the Dumpster. But there was no sign of the girl. I tried not to imagine her shivering and looking for a place to sleep. The thought of it made me feel like I'd eaten too much.

Dad tied up a bag of garbage and propped it against the wall.

"Yoo-hoo! Knock knock! Y'all want some company? I've got something for you to taste-test." Bibi had come up the stairs and was banging on the apartment door.

"Come on in," my mother said. She waddled out of the kitchen and opened the door.

"My goodness, what an evening! All that smoke in the air! Feels sort of like my lungs have been charbroiled!" Bibi slipped her sneakers off and, using her foot, gently swept them under the coat rack.

I loved Bibi and the funny things she said. Sometimes I didn't know if she was being serious or just crazy silly. About six years ago, she had moved up north from someplace down south, renting an apartment just a couple of blocks from us.

"Less snakes and frizz-free hair," Bibi had told me was the reason she had settled in East Thumb. By now she must have learned that we have frizzy hair up here. And snakes, too. I had seen one slither under the Dumpster more than once.

Bibi loved to bake, and my parents never said no to her

desserts when she brought them into the diner. I'd highlight them on the blackboard with the other specials—Bibi's snickerdoodles, Bibi's whoopie pies, or Bibi's whatever—depending on what goodie she felt like whipping up. Sometimes I'd go to her apartment and bake with her. On those times, she always made sure the blackboard said my name, not hers. "Lizzy's dessert today!" She'd tell the customers, even when I had only cracked the eggs and measured flour.

"Smells good," my dad said. "What have you got there? Something made with cinnamon, I know that."

"You've got a good nose for sweets, Henry." Bibi carried a tray of sticky buns into the kitchen.

She unbuttoned her furry coat using her free hand. "Don't you worry, this ain't real," she said to me. "It's high-quality fake. Feel it, come on." She held an elbow out for me.

"I believe you," I said. I patted the fur tentatively with my hand.

"I know y'all are big animal lovers. I wouldn't traipse in here with a real fur even if I could afford one."

"That's good to know," I said. Real fur coats made me sad when I thought about how they got to be coats.

"Let's go into the living room," my mother suggested. Bibi's black hair was out of its usual ponytail that she wore to work. It was pushed off her forehead with a wide headband and the ends flipped up a little bit like buffalo horns, which bounced as she followed my parents down the hall.

She held the tray out to us. "These buns are *dan-ger-ous*—they are so good. I've got two dozen more I'll bring into the diner tomorrow. If I don't eat them all up myself. Please! Somebody stop me, if I try!"

My mother pulled a tiny piece off of one. "I'm going to save the rest for breakfast."

I knew she was just being polite. And Bibi knew my mother well enough now, too, to know that Mom wouldn't eat a sticky bun for breakfast or anytime, actually, ever since she became pregnant and turned into a way healthier eater than she used to be.

Dad pushed a big hunk into his mouth.

"I'll have one," I said. It was warm and sticky when I scooped it up.

Another bun slipped off the tray. Dad held his hand out and caught it before it hit the floor.

"Oops! Nice save," I said.

"Thanks. I guess that calls for seconds."

I could see by Mom's face she wasn't too happy about that, given the conversation we had just had at dinner. But I couldn't blame Dad. When a sticky bun falls into your hand, that's a no-brainer sign to eat it.

Bibi put the tray down on the coffee table, and when everyone took a seat, I headed back to the kitchen window to check again for the girl. Would she at least find the bag and the Coke I had left for her?

"Listen here," I heard Bibi say to my parents as soon as I stepped out of the room. I stopped. She continued in a whispery voice, "I chatted with Sergeant Blumstein for a bit outside, and he implied that the fire might be no accident."

"Is that so," my father said.

No accident? I took a step back toward the living room.

"I guess something like that is always a possibility," my father continued. "But the building is old and battered. Even without an accelerant, I bet it would have blazed up very quickly."

Waffles sat a few feet away by the back door. He barked several times to go out. But I didn't move. My brain was still processing what I had just heard.

"Lizzy? You taking the dog out?" Mom hollered.

"I'll do it," Dad said before I could answer. "I want to dump the garbage." I scrambled back down the hall into the kitchen so Dad wouldn't catch me eavesdropping. I heard the metal part of the leash bang against the wall when Dad lifted it off its little hook. "Let's go, big guy."

When my feet could move again, I made my way to my room. My bedroom shared a wall with the living room, and I could hear bits of conversation about the weather, and a "to die for" sweater

Bibi had just bought and was gushing about. Nothing more about the fire. Suddenly, I felt exhausted. I plopped onto my bed. I had a great view out my window of all the action still going on outside. After a few seconds, the flashing lights bothered my eyes, and I dropped my shade.

I reached for my cell phone to text Joss, but she beat me to it. It buzzed in my hand.

Did u see the girl?

No. But Bibi came over and told us the fire was set on purpose

OMG really????

I told Joss about finding Smoky and everything I knew.

You think the girl did it?

Maybe. Do U?

IDK. Why would she? She gone for good?

Probs. 🙁

🙁

"Looking for this?" Dad poked his head into my room. He held up my bag.

"Oh, thanks," I said. He dropped it gently on my floor. Before he closed the door, Smoky tore through his legs and sprang onto my bed. "How about that. Making himself right at home already."

Before he could shut the door, I yelled out, "Wait!"

"What?"

"Where's my Coke? Did you throw it out?"

"What Coke?"

"The cup I left outside next to my bag. I forgot that, too."

"Well, you must have forgot that someplace else. There was no Coke. Just the bag." Then he cupped his ear and tilted his head upward.

"Hear that?" he asked me.

"What?"

"It's a sticky bun calling my name." He made the Vulcan salute and left.

I jumped up and grabbed my bag. I turned it upside down. Four pencils, my notebook, a pink eraser, and two already wished-on wishbones spilled out. That was it. The food was gone. But, probably, so was the girl.

CHAPTER 7

IT TOOK A POODLE, A CAT, AND A STICKY BUN TO find her. Waffles's barking woke me, but I was sort of already waking, anyway, trying to escape a bad dream.

I sat up, but the dream was still inside my head. *The siren wailed. Dad's face glowed bright blue.* That's the image I always remember. My dad's blue face when the lights of the police car showed up behind us.

I squeezed my eyes shut while the dream floated out of my reach like a lost balloon. My heart thumped and my nightgown stuck to my back with sweat. I pulled it away from my skin and kicked the covers off. One thirty was technically morning, but way too early to be up. Though my pets didn't seem to mind.

Enough moonlight seeped through my shade so I could see that Smoky was perched on top of my dresser, and Waffles jumped and yapped at him. The cat seemed amused and took a couple of swipes at the dog, but missed. I got out of bed and stepped on Waffles's favorite toy, a well-chewed stuffed owl with an eye missing, just like him. It squeaked under my foot. At the sound, Waffles grabbed it in his mouth and trotted out of my room. Now I was wide awake and hungry.

In the kitchen, I ate a sticky bun, which made me thirsty. Smoky was following me, and he rubbed his head on my calf while I waited at the sink for the water to run cold. It was pitch-black outside the window. Then, I saw the light go on inside the Enterprise. I saw the back of her head and that red hair. I was so surprised, I turned the faucet off fast, like she could hear it. I didn't want to startle her and have her run off again. Duh, like she had superpower hearing or something. I shut the kitchen light off, just in case. I didn't want her to know she'd been seen. That might make her run. I wanted to know who she was. Why she had to sleep in my father's truck. Why she hadn't run away from here, after all. She was writing in something. A notebook . . . ? A diary? I couldn't tell.

I grabbed a sticky bun and a napkin. Maybe she had eaten most of the food by now. Then I threw my coat on, stuffed my feet into a pair of boots, and quietly raced down the stairs and outside.

She jumped when I tapped on the passenger side window. Her first instinct was to shut the light off. But then she quickly pushed it on again as if it had registered in her mind that it was me and not anyone else. The wind blew. I got a whiff of the burned apartment building, and I shivered as I felt the cold bite at my bare legs. The girl stared back at me through the truck window as if not knowing what to do. Her face was pale, like a glass of milk. Her cheekbones were sharp and high, jutting out under two of the greenest eyes I'd ever seen. I walked around to the driver's side where she was sitting and opened the truck door.

"Hi. I brought you something," I said. I offered her the sticky bun.

"Thanks." She took it and pushed almost half of it into her mouth. She closed her eyes when she chewed, like it was the best thing she'd ever tasted in her whole life.

"Good, isn't it?"

"OMG," she said, licking her fingers. "Thanks for all the food. I already ate most of it. I guess running away makes me hungry." She turned and looked back up at my apartment. "Your parents don't know about me, do they?"

"No. They don't know about you at all." Though it crossed my mind right then that they, too, could have seen her on the news. "I saw you through the kitchen window when I got up to get a drink of water."

"I didn't know where else to sleep," she said.

"That's fine. I hope it's . . . comfortable. . . ."

"It's better than sleeping under an overpass."

"Really?"

"Well, yeah!" The girl looked surprised, like, why wouldn't I know that the inside of a truck was way better than sleeping under a bridge?

"I meant, *really* you've slept under an overpass? Not, *really* was the truck more comfortable."

"Oh," she said, shaking her head. "No, I didn't sleep under an overpass, I'm just saying this truck was a better option than that."

"And a burning house," I added.

She blinked a few times without saying anything, and then said, "Yeah, that too."

"How old are you?" I asked her.

"Eleven," she said. "How about you?"

"Oh," I said. Suddenly, she looked even smaller. And her hair, not so much spiky and cool in the front, but just a mess.

"What?" she asked.

"Nothing. I thought you were older." That made her smile. "I'm twelve," I added. "And just so you know, my dad gets up at four thirty to get ready for work. I think it's close to two or something," I told her.

"Okay," she said, finishing the bun. "I should just leave now and look for a new place to hide." She grabbed her bag and grasped the steering wheel with her free hand, sliding herself off the seat. The truck was pretty high. I stepped forward and offered her my hand. What had Bibi said about sticking your hand out when someone needs it? The girl took it and hoisted herself out and down. That's when I got a good look at the little green tattoo drawn on her hand. A clover. But not a regular plain old clover. It had four leaves!

"Your tattoo!" I said. I felt the hair stand up on the back of my neck. I was already practically freezing to death, and my teeth were chattering. But this was a different chill.

"What about it?"

"It's . . . good luck."

"*Pffffftttt!*" she said. "I wish. I'm going."

"Where? Where are you going to go?" I asked.

"I can't stay in your dad's truck," she said.

"I know, but what are you going to do? Where do you think you will go?" I was staring at the thing on her hand. Was this a sign? A sign that she was good luck? If she was lucky, and she stayed around, maybe I wouldn't have to worry about something bad happening to Mom again.

"Thanks for that awesome cinnamon bun," she was saying. "I probably won't see you after tonight. Maybe I can find another empty house."

All those worries about Mom spilled out of my brain and piled up inside me like a tall stack of pancakes. "Wait!" I said to her, before she had the chance to walk away. "I saw you on the news today. Well, my friend did. People are looking for you. But I can hide you. I can keep you in my room." The words just shot out of my mouth. It was too late to catch them and shove them back inside. "Then you could have a warm place to sleep every night and food. . . . I could bring it to you easily. . . . My parents are at the diner a lot." A tiny bubble of fear fizzled inside my belly. But sneaking this stranger into my house could not have been scarier than what this poor girl must have been feeling not knowing where she was going to hide. And she was only eleven! I needed to bring her inside where she would be safe.

She stared at me. It dawned on me that I was a stranger to her, too. She must have been scared. But she shrugged her shoulders and said, "Okay."

"What's your name?" I asked.

"Charlotte," she told me.

When I first saw her, I would have guessed she had a name like Jade or Willow, or something edgy like that. But now, she definitely seemed more like a Charlotte.

"What? Are you thinking that it's creepy to be named after a spider?"

"Not at all. I loved *Charlotte's Web*," I said. "Besides, Charlotte wasn't just any old spider. She was a hero. And brave. And really smart. And resourceful. Did your mom like that book or something?"

"It was her favorite to read when she was young. And ever since, Charlotte was always her favorite name."

Maybe her mother shouted out lines from *Charlotte's Web* like "Terrific!" or "Some Pig!" like my dad did with the Star Trek stuff. Maybe we had that in common.

"Come on. Let's go. Don't forget that." I pointed to the book she'd been writing in that was still on the front seat.

"I won't." She reached in and grabbed it. Then, slowly, she closed the truck door, pushing it gently into place with both hands so as not to make a slamming sound.

"Stay behind me." I grabbed her by the hand, guiding her to the door that led to our apartment. I pulled her inside.

"Watch your step."

We immediately began to climb the stairs. "Wait here, while I check to see if the coast is clear," I whispered, when we reached the door at the top. I stepped into the front hall. I tiptoed by the kitchen, and into a back hall that led to my parents' bedroom. Waffles came from behind me, bumped up against my leg, and licked my hand. My parents' door was open, and I could see the outline of their bodies. I could tell from the sound of their breathing that they were both still sound asleep. I hurried back, took Charlotte's hand, and led her to my room.

"I hope you don't mind dogs," I whispered. "He's super friendly." Waffles had followed us and was all over Charlotte, angling for a back rub or whatever attention he could get.

"He's so cute," Charlotte said, "like a lamb." His tail wagged like crazy while Charlotte petted the top of his head.

I rearranged some of the things in my closet, moving shoes, books, and a jewelry box out of the way. I grabbed an extra blanket off my closet shelf and the afghan Joss had knitted me for my birthday last year from the end of my bed. I laid the blankets out on the closet floor, creating a cozy space for sleeping. Then I handed her a couple of throw pillows.

"Ta da!" I said softly. I held my arms out toward my closet, welcoming Charlotte to her new home. "Your new closet. But it's a lot better than the old one, right?"

"Definitely." She smiled. She dropped her bag inside. "Your room smells like pancakes. Or is it french fries? Grilled cheese?" Charlotte took a big whiff. "Does your house always smell this good?"

"Probably. But I'm so used to it, I don't smell anything. It's from the diner. Downstairs."

"I'd be hungry all the time living up here."

"You'd get used to it, too."

"That's so cool that your house comes with its own diner."

Funny. In all the years we've lived here, which was my whole life, I never thought of it that way. *A house with its very own diner.* Maybe because we had to go outside to the back of the diner to get inside our home upstairs, it didn't really feel like the same house, more like just an ordinary apartment upstairs. But actually, Charlotte was right. I did live in a house with its very own diner, and suddenly, it felt a little more special.

"Good night," Charlotte said. "Well, good morning technically, but good night, anyway." She curled up, tucked both pillows under her head, and closed her eyes. I shut the closet almost the whole way.

I climbed back into bed with my heart racing. I had just moved a total stranger into my room. There was something very thrilling about the thought. Because while I'm positive it's never ever a safe thing to let a stranger sleep in your closet, it felt really good that I was helping someone. And very cool that I had a secret. And, possibly, a new friend, who, if I was reading the sign right, would turn out to be a real live good luck charm.

CHAPTER
8

IT TURNED OUT, NEITHER OF US COULD ACTUALLY sleep. The smell of the diner had made Charlotte hungry again; plus, Waffles stayed around and took up so much space on my bed I couldn't get comfortable. So we (Waffles, too) ended up finishing off a bag of Dad's potato chips and staying up for a while longer talking about a bunch of things, including the fire.

"Did you smell the smoke right away?"

"Yes. And I could taste it," Charlotte told me.

"Weren't you scared to death? I would have been, like, freaking out. . . ."

"I was. It was the scariest thing ever. I just grabbed my bag and Smoky and ran. I didn't even try to go out the front. I could see the fire was burning from that direction. I went through the kitchen and out the back door."

Charlotte was lucky the back door hadn't been boarded up like the front door had!

She had seen Joss and me outside when the fire trucks had shown up. We had been right. Charlotte had ignored us on purpose so we wouldn't call attention to her. She had slipped away into the crowd, then hid in the bushes behind one of the other apartment houses on Greenleaf.

"That's when Smoky took off. I'm glad that you found him," she said. "Or, that he found you." Charlotte explained that later on, once the streets had emptied out, she looked for a car or truck she could sleep in. She didn't have to look for long. Dad's truck, the Enterprise, was only her second try. East Thumb was the kind of town where most people never felt the need to lock their doors.

"I had a cute cat once," she told me in a quiet voice. "And nice parents." She had a sister and a brother, too, twins Molly and Ethan, who were seven. They were the reason she had left a note behind when she ran away. "Otherwise I wouldn't even have done that. But I knew they would be scared, so I did. My little brother, especially. He's scared of everything. He sometimes makes me sit at the end of his bed until he falls asleep."

Besides the fact that my bedroom was dark, I couldn't see Charlotte at all because the closet door was almost shut. But her voice sounded like it came out of a sad face. I wanted to ask her a thousand questions, but I was nervous to hear her answers, because if they were bad, I might not know the right things to say. So I waited for her to say more. And then she did.

"My dad is leaving us."

"Where's he going?" I asked.

"I have no idea. He doesn't want to live with us anymore."

"That stinks," I said.

"I know. It's mean, right? And the weirdest, most stupidest thing is my mom seems glad about it. Isn't that dumb?" She stuck her head out the closet door. I sat up in bed and turned toward her shadowy face. "My parents fight a lot," she said. "More than a lot. It's always about stupid stuff. It's so stupid!" She sniffed in, and I could tell that she was crying. "Right before I ran away, my parents told me that my dad was moving out. It just made me so mad that they both could think it was okay for him to leave us. What did we do wrong? So I left first."

I sucked in my breath like I had touched something hot.

"Now my dad knows how it feels to have someone run out on *him*. Maybe he'll change his mind. Maybe my mom won't think it's so okay." She hiccupped as if she had swallowed too many tears and they had gone down the wrong way. "I even left my cell phone home so they couldn't track me."

Charlotte was, like, the bravest person I knew. It took guts to run away. More guts than I'd ever have. I sometimes got scared just walking in the dark to use the bathroom at night.

"I bet your dad will change his mind," I said. "How long are you planning to stay away?"

"I'm not sure," she said, yawning. Her head disappeared back inside the closet.

"How come you came to East Thumb?" I asked her.

"Twelve dollars."

"Twelve dollars?"

"Yeah. That's every cent I had. I bought the ticket that would take me the farthest away from Lewiston. And . . ." She stopped for a second. "And that's how I ended up here," she said.

But it sounded like she was going to say something else. I wanted to ask her more about the fire. I couldn't get what Bibi had said about it being set on purpose out of my head. But I didn't want to sound like I was thinking she had set it. The way she described what had happened sounded like she had been totally surprised, anyways.

I heard the sound of her breathing. There was a soft exhale every few seconds, and I knew she had fallen asleep.

I laid back down and pulled my quilt up against my face. Then I fell asleep thinking about the fact that one minute Charlotte had been hiding out in the closet of that burned down apartment house. And now she was hiding out in mine.

● ● ●

I woke up wondering how I was going to keep Charlotte a secret from my parents. Last night I hadn't thought about things like how she would get to the bathroom without being seen or heard. Or what she was supposed to do when I was at school all day and my mom was home, at least some of that time, when she was taking breaks from the diner.

I pulled the shade away from my window. The sun sucker punched me in the face. In the bright daylight, the burned apartment house looked even worse. Half of the building was still standing. Part of the roof still covered some of the top floor, but the front of the house had been completely burned away. I could see the walls and rooms inside like a giant ruined dollhouse.

There were large blackened pieces of floor that arched down toward the ground like charred waterfalls. Chunks of broken house covered the sidewalk. The big tree that just yesterday was full of faded leaves was black in several places, its branches completely bare. Everything looked dark and doomed. A police car and a red car, probably from the fire department, were parked near the curb.

I flung my covers off. It was after nine o'clock. Working at the diner on Sundays was optional for me. Today, I had more important things to do than bus tables. Joss and I were picking out yarn for the cat sweaters. And of course there was the matter of Charlotte. And keeping her out of sight.

I walked quietly to my closet and peeked into the small gap of space.

Charlotte was curled up on her side in a ball, the blankets tucked under one arm and pushed against her nose. At some point in the night, Smoky had slipped in. He was snuggled next to her, a paw resting against her knees. Waffles was sprawled out on the floor sleeping by the closet door.

I found the girl she's in my closet asleep, I texted Joss.

JK? Joss texted back.

No I'm not kidding I'm serious

???????????????????

I found her hiding in my dad's truck. I snuck her in when my parents were sleeping

WHAAAAAATTTT?????

BTW my parents don't know OBVI so shhhhhhh

How's that gonna work?

IDK

Did she say anything about the fire?

Yes she smelled smoke and ran

Mom was up. I could hear her moving around in the kitchen. I set the phone down and checked Charlotte one more time. She was still sound asleep. Being a runaway had to be exhausting. Plus, we were up most of the night, too.

In the kitchen, Mom measured coffee into the coffee maker.

"Hi," I said.

"Hi, love," Mom said to me over her shoulder. "You coming to work with me today?"

"Nah. I've got stuff to do."

"Homework?"

"Sort of." If *working*-on-hiding-a-stranger-in-your-*home* equals homework.

Mom leaned against the counter while the coffee brewed. I sat down at the table.

"Elle is taking Joss and me to the Yarn Barn in Portland today," I said.

"That's right."

I had told Mom this already, but pregnancy makes you forget stuff. Still, Mom's face seemed brighter, and she looked more rested than usual. Lately, she looked tired most days even when she had just woken up, since her big belly made it hard for her to sleep soundly sometimes. Maybe Charlotte's good luck had kicked in already!

"You be sure to let me know when a couple of sweaters are available for Fudge and Smoky. You know Reuben won't want to wear a sweater, so . . ."

"I know," I said.

"Dad and I are happy to help you girls raise some money. We're so proud of you, Lizzy."

"Thanks," I said. "Can you believe the apartment house? Did you see what's left of it? It's ruined."

"I saw. It will have to be torn down. There'll be a big empty lot over there now," she said. "Gosh."

"What do you think happened? Last night I heard Bibi say it was set on purpose."

"Oh." Mom looked surprised that I had overheard their conversation, but then seemed to not care at all that I had. "Well, she didn't really say *that*. She said the police are *wondering* if it was set on purpose." Mom poured herself coffee and stirred in some milk. She wore a dark gray sweater that stretched across her tummy like she was hiding a basketball underneath.

"Why would someone start a fire on purpose?" I asked.

"If they wanted to cause some trouble, I guess. Or, maybe they did it for money."

"Money?"

"It looks like the owner of the house hadn't taken care of those apartments in quite some time. They weren't in any condition to be rented out."

"What does that have to do with burning a house down on purpose for money?"

Mom explained about houses having insurance. Like cars. If you get into a car accident, insurance pays to fix your car. Or gives you money to put toward a new one.

"Did they do that for our accident?" I asked. And then I was sorry I did. Mom didn't like to talk about the car accident. None of us did.

She nodded. "And if something happens to a house, like a fire, insurance will cover that, too."

"So they set their own house on fire to collect the insurance money?"

"I really don't think that's the case." Mom sipped her coffee. "That's a very bad thing. Illegal," she continued. "But . . . desperate people do desperate things. Sometimes bad things. There. Now you have a lesson in arson and ripping off insurance companies." She gave me a goofy smile as if she had told me too much about something I didn't need to know. "But Lizzy," she said, tucking her hair behind her ear, "that's just based on gossip. The real truth is probably something else—an old wire, or maybe as Dad said, someone burning leaves too close by."

That reminded me of the dried-up leaves that blew around our feet yesterday while Joss and I stood on the porch. *Trouble was swirling,* I had thought at the time. Um . . . *yeah!* You think??

"Since you're not working with me today, let's have breakfast together," Mom said.

"What do you feel like?" I asked. "I'll make something."

"Why do that when we can have someone else cook and clean up?"

Because there's a stranger in my closet and I'm not sure I should leave right now. "We don't want to hog two diner seats on a Sunday morning," I said.

"Of course we do. You and I? Go get dressed," she told me. "I'm craving one of Dad's veggie omelets."

Back in my room, Charlotte still slept. I pulled on my jeans and dropped a sweater over my head. I grabbed a pen and scribbled a note to Charlotte, explaining how long I'd be gone, when Mom and Dad would be home, and to help herself to something to eat.

I placed it next to her and got a close-up look at that four-leaf clover on her hand.

I thought about all the ways Charlotte had been lucky even if she probably didn't think so. Lucky that Joss and I had gone looking for that cat. Lucky that she had escaped from the fire. And lucky that Smoky and Waffles woke me up last night so that I could sneak her inside my house.

Charlotte twitched lightly, but she kept on sleeping.

I hoped she would stay for a while. Long enough to spread lots of luckiness around here. Maybe even long enough for a baby to be born.

CHAPTER 9

IT WAS CLOSE TO ELEVEN WHEN JOSS AND HER sister, Elle, picked me up outside the diner. As soon as I got into the car, Joss sent me a text, even though I was sitting in the back seat right behind her.

What's up with the girl?

Her name is Charlotte and that tattoo on her hand is a 4 leaf clover

Really?

It's such a total sign! She's good luck!

Cool but it's not a real tattoo

Duh. But it's still a 4 leaf clover! That's always a sign of good luck no matter what

I guess

In the ten minutes it took to get to Portland, I texted Joss pretty much everything I hadn't had a chance to tell her yet about Charlotte.

Elle found a parking spot in the Old Port. "I've got a bunch of stuff to do. Mom said to feed you guys," she said. "Want to meet at Butter & Jam Café in an hour? We can get croissants, or whatever."

"Sure," I said, even though I had just eaten a stack of pancakes.

"Cool," Joss told her sister.

"Okay, I'll see you in a little bit." Elle crossed the street, and Joss and I walked the three blocks to the Yarn Barn.

"So what's the rest of Charlotte's story?"

"I texted you everything I know. She was still asleep when I left this morning."

"You don't think she'll be gone when you get home later, do you?"

I stopped walking. Suddenly, I felt like I needed a deep breath. "Why would she leave? She just got here."

"I don't know." Joss shrugged. "Maybe she'll have second thoughts about hiding out in your house. Maybe she wants to go home. I mean, I know she's mad at her dad, but you made it sound like she feels pretty bad leaving her brother and sister."

I stood on the sidewalk in a kind of mini trance. *A lucky charm comes into my life and quickly disappears.* That would be an awful sign.

"Quit trying to analyze everything all the time," Joss said as if she was reading my mind. She grabbed my arm and pulled me along. "Even if she is gone when you get home, nothing bad will happen, okay? You're going to drive yourself nuts trying to figure out how to control everything before it happens."

"I'm not."

"Nuts? Or trying to control everything?"

"Either," I said. "You just think about things differently than I do. It's hard for you to understand."

"It's not that hard. Trust me."

"Well, you know what's hard?" I asked. We stopped walking again, and Joss looked at me. "Finding a four-leaf clover. I searched it on the Internet, and it's like a one in ten thousand chance."

"Um . . . hello . . . Charlotte's tattoo didn't grow out of her lawn, Lizzy."

"Exactly. Finding one on the lawn is just plain lucky. But finding one on *someone* . . . that's something else. It means something. It's a sign that if she sticks around she can bring me good luck. Plus, I didn't just find her once, I found her twice. What are the odds of that?"

Joss didn't say anything. She started walking again.

"Maybe Charlotte will stay until the baby is born," I continued, catching up with her. "Do you think she'd stay away from her family that long? I mean, she really seems angry at her dad. Not just a little bit."

Joss sighed. "Lizzy, your mom—I mean, the baby—it's all going to be okay this time." She reached up and adjusted my scarf, which had started to unravel. "And you really can't control everything. I don't just mean *you*; I mean, no one can. Otherwise there would never be anything bad happening in the world, right?"

"I think we can control some things sometimes. We just need to pay closer attention."

"To . . . ?"

"Everything."

"Well, you can pay attention, I guess, but you still can't control your whole life. Even if there are . . . 'signs.'" Joss pumped her fingers like quotation marks. "I mean, if you really honestly believe that . . . but they can't tell you everything you want to know. That's just impossible."

We'd had this conversation more than a few times.

"You be you and I'll be me, okay?" I said. "You think what you want. But I don't always have to agree."

"I know," Joss said. Which is how this topic always ended.

At the yarn store, picking colors was hard. There were so many to choose from. Some had flecks in them or different shades of the same color all in one ball.

"In this bin over here, you're going to get your best price," the lady told us. "I suggest you choose from that lot. Cats aren't going to care if they're wearing wool or acrylic, are they?" She laughed.

"I guess not," Joss told her. "But our customers might."

"Well, those yarns are soft enough for a baby's blanket. They should work very nicely. You can choose what you want. I'm just saying, I can offer you the steepest discount on those acrylics, understand?" she said, before walking away to help another customer.

"Joss, I think those will work. We can't afford expensive wool. And she's giving us a big break on the price of this stuff." I pointed to the bin piled high with yarn.

"I know, but wool is nicer."

"Wool is itchy. And a homeless cat has enough problems, don't you think? Plus, the idea is to raise money. And the less expensive the yarn, the more we make for the Lodge."

"Okay. I guess." She sounded borderline grumpy about it.

"I know you're the knitting expert here," I said, trying to butter her up. "But I know a thing or two about running a business." That really wasn't true *exactly*, but with all the time I spent in the diner helping out and all the conversations I'd overheard about profit margins, and operation expenses, it felt true-ish. "You stick to production and I'll stick to the money side of stuff, okay?"

Joss nodded.

"And let's stay away from pinks and baby blues, because some people are funny about what they'll dress their boy or girl cats in and we don't want to knit more of one color than it turns out we need or can sell," I added. I was impressed with how much sense I was making. Maybe I had more business savvy than I thought.

"You're right," Joss agreed, and her smile was back.

I grabbed one of the metal carry baskets and dropped in some green and gray yarns.

"What about knitting needles?" I asked. Joss was going to reteach me how to knit.

"I have plenty of extras at home," she said.

"Okay. Maybe you can show Charlotte, too? It will give her something to do while she hangs out in my closet."

"Sure."

Joss's grandmother had taught her how to knit. After Joss had given me lessons, I made an afghan with some extra holes in it, and a few pairs of mittens with super huge thumbs. Joss told me that knitting wasn't my forte. I had to Google what forte meant, but basically, it meant that I stunk at it. So I was a little nervous to pick it up again, because I didn't like not being good at something.

Up at the register, I counted out the money our parents had given us to get the fund-raiser started. We were also each donating some of our own money that we had earned from working at the diner.

Thanks to the big discount the lady was giving us, we could

buy enough yarn to make at least thirty sweaters and have money left over to buy poster board for the signs we needed to make to tell people about the sale. The lady bagged our yarn and then handed us another sack. Inside was more yarn!

"Consider this a donation for a good cause," she said.

"Thanks!" we both said at the same time.

"I like kids who like good causes. And I like cats. You have a good day."

"You too," we told her.

"Thanks again," Joss said. We both waved as we headed toward the door. I held it open for Joss and followed her outside.

"See! Charlotte *is* good luck!" I said, when we stepped back out on the street. "How lucky is getting a bag full of free yarn?"

"Or . . ." Joss brought her nose so close to mine they almost bumped. "Or . . . ," she said again, "it was just because the yarn lady was super nice. And she likes cats." Joss pulled her face back from mine and raised her eyebrows.

"*Or*"—I said, tipping my head side to side as I said each word in a big voice—"It. Was. Good. Luck."

"How about both?"

"Okay," I said, dropping my head back and lifting my face toward the sun. "Both!" I yelled out. The sky was a Popsicle blue. The kind of Popsicle that tasted like raspberry, which I never understood, because raspberries are pink. A white puffy turtle cloud hovered above us. *Take it slow*? Could that have to do with Charlotte?

"Look at that cloud. It's a ladybug," Joss said, pointing at it.

"Oh yeah, it could be a ladybug," I said. And maybe it was! That would be better than a turtle. I was pretty sure ladybugs were a sign of good luck.

We stopped at Walgreens to get poster board. Then we walked around the Old Port. On Commercial Street, Joss found a pizza crust on the sidewalk and tossed it to the seagulls on one of the piers. We tried on earrings at our favorite store, Hoopla-la. Up on Market Street a lady was handing out samples of a "farmhouse" cheddar in front of the Fermented Cow Cheese Shop.

"Do you have just regular american cheese? Preferably orange?" Joss asked her. She shook her head no. I didn't mind the cheese, but when we were out of sight, Joss spit her free sample into a trash can. "Gross," she said.

On Fore Street, we stopped at Maxwell's to smell soaps and candles. We had a find-the-funniest-birthday-card contest at Card & Paper. We bought three tubes of lip balm at Pucker Up. "Hopefully, Charlotte likes cherry," I said.

On our way to the café, I found a quarter on Wharf Street wedged between two cobblestones. How many lucky things had happened already since Charlotte had arrived? I was sure today had been luckier than usual.

"*Hello!*" I said, waving the coin in front of Joss's face.

It crossed my mind that luck was a lot like a total stranger. It could pop into your life like Charlotte did. It could be good. Or not so good.

That's why you had to pay attention. Look for the signs. If you read them right, it made all the difference between lucky and *almost* lucky. And nobody wants to be *almost* lucky. Because almost lucky isn't lucky at all.

CHAPTER
10

BY ONE THIRTY, WE WERE BACK IN THE CAR, HEAD-
ing home to East Thumb. I wiped at a spot on my jeans. I had
pulled my croissant into two pieces to save half for Charlotte and
had made a small mess.

"When's the baby due?" Elle asked.

"Pretty soon," I told her. I brushed slivers of almond off the
back seat. "About seven more weeks."

"Good." She smiled at me in the rearview mirror . . . one of
those "baby" smiles that had other things behind them. It was a
little bit sad, or nervous, just never straight-out happy.

"So, tomorrow I have to drive you guys to school?" Elle asked.
"I should start charging. Maybe I get a cut in your cat sweater
thing."

"Umm . . . it's a *fund-raiser*." Joss made a face at her sister.

"Umm . . . it's a joke," Elle said.

Joss turned and asked me over the front seat, "Is Smoky ready for his modeling debut?"

"I hope so. He better not get stage fright in front of the class. Maybe I should put the sweater on him before we get him to school?"

"No. We need to demonstrate for the class how easy it is to put one on," Joss said.

"Who is Smoky, anyway?" Elle asked. "Never heard of that cat."

I explained how he was a stray cat we brought in. "Fudge was going to be our original sweater model . . . he's so super laid-back, but Smoky is fresh off the streets. He's all skinny and everything. He's a better example of why our fund-raiser is so important. Plus, he seems laid-back, too. He's not even scared of Waffles or the other cats."

Elle pulled up in front of the Community Lodge for Cats & Dogs. Franny had suggested we give each person who buys a cat sweater a free window decal with the shelter's logo on it. We were picking up the decals today since we planned on taking sweater orders tomorrow after the demonstration with Smoky. Plus, Joss and I wanted to show Franny all the yarn that we had picked out.

"Hurry up," Elle told us. "I'll wait in the car."

"You don't want to come in?" I asked.

"It makes me sad," she said. I could understand that. It was probably for the same reason it made me sad sometimes, too—wondering if the animals thought they were here because no one loved them.

Beyond the parking lot were the kennels for the dogs. The outdoor spaces were neat and clean and covered with green tarps. The whole area was surrounded by a chain-link fence and then divided into fenced sections so two or three dogs shared a dog-house and a good-sized space.

A hound with long floppy ears pressed his nose against the fence. Three terriers, all mixed with some other breed, barked and wagged their little tails.

"I know, we love you, too," Joss told them as we passed by.

"We do. We love you!" I said.

We had never actually adopted any of our pets from a shelter like Joss's Marco, who came from the Lodge. All of our pets had been strays, living on the streets. They could have been shelter pets if we hadn't found each other first.

The shelter's office and the cats were located next to the kennels inside a building that looked like a small house. The lobby was cramped with the front counter taking up most of the space, and it smelled kind of stinky from the animals, but I didn't mind.

Mounted on the wall was a giant whiteboard that kept track

of new arrivals, vet appointments, and who was working on which day. Keys, leashes, and collars in all different sizes hung from hooks everywhere.

Inside, a few visitors filled out paperwork while others waited to see a cat or dog.

"Hey there," Franny said to us from behind the counter.

Phil, one of the managers, was busy beside her. "Hey," he said when he saw us. Phil had a silver ring in his nose and his hair was dyed blue. Some days his hair was green, sometimes orange, one time it was gray like an old man's, which looked kind of funny because he didn't seem *that* old.

Franny's hair was gray all the time, and she wore it in a long braid down her back. She always wore tank tops, even in the winter, usually with the name of some rock band I'd never heard of on the front of it. Zuma, Franny's giant Maine coon cat, was stretched out and sound asleep on top of the counter.

"I've got those decals for you," she said, handing me a stack held together with a rubber band. They were white, the size of a baseball, with a black paw print in the middle. The Lodge's name and phone number were on it, but instead of an *O* in the word lodge there was a small red heart.

"Thanks. These are nice," I said, showing Joss. "The little heart is a sign that everyone will love our sweaters."

"Really?" she said, then to Franny and Phil, "Look at the yarn we bought for the cat sweaters." She held up a few balls. "Do you like the colors we chose?"

"Really wonderful!" Franny said.

"Nice," Phil said. "I hope the cats like them."

Someone filling out a form looked up.

"My cat Fudge would wear anything," I told him.

"Good for you girls," Franny said. "I'm sure many cats will appreciate a cozy sweater."

I saw Phil raise his eyebrows a bit before he motioned to a lady, then led her into the cat room.

"We bought stuff to make posters to advertise the fund-raiser, too," I said. "We don't have time to make one now. Joss's sister is waiting for us. But we'll be back later this week to put one up."

"Thank you, girls. You're the best. Take a quick peek at the new kittens that just arrived."

We stuffed the yarn back inside the bags. Then we looked into the cat room, which was separated from the lobby by a door with a window halfway up.

Metal cat cages lined two of the walls. Each cage had the cat's name, a blanket, food and water, and a small pan of litter inside. But the cats spent a lot of time roaming free in the room. Except for the one or two cats whose cages were marked NOT SOCIAL because they either didn't get along with the others or they had a health issue. They had separate "free time."

The lady with Phil kneeled by the kittens, who were snuggled together on a blanket in a furry clump. Only one was awake, grabbing at another's little tail with its paw. Two were orange tabbies and two were black with just a white patch of fur on their chins.

"They're so little," Joss said.

"I want to hold one," I said, feeling a pinch in my chest.

"Not now," Joss said, pulling my arm. "Elle will get mad if we make her wait long, and we need her to drive us to school tomorrow."

I nodded. I needed to get home for Charlotte, too.

"See you next time," Franny said, and we waved good-bye.

Back in the car, Elle refused to make another stop for us since she had already driven us to Portland, the shelter, and, now, back to my house.

"Why won't you just stop home first so I can grab my knitting needles?" Joss begged.

"You've hit your ride quota for the day. You're lucky you have all those bags to carry or I would have made you guys walk from the shelter."

"Your house is just a five-minute walk to my house," I told Joss.

"Fine. I'll *walk* over after I get my stuff," Joss said.

"You got that right," Elle told her.

• • •

The diner was still full of customers at two o'clock when Elle dropped me off. Through the big front windows I saw Mom and Bibi, each for a split second, rushing around. I scooted by quickly so they wouldn't see me and wave me inside. I wanted to get back to Charlotte right away.

The sun was flashlight-in-your-eyes bright. Twigs and acorn caps snapped and crunched under my boots when I booked it down the alley to my apartment. I raced upstairs and straight to my bedroom. The closet was wide open and empty.

"Charlotte?" I hollered, dropping the bags of yarn and poster board. My chest tightened up and squeezed the breath out of me.

"I'm in here," she said.

I jogged to the living room. Charlotte was sitting on the couch. The TV was on, but the volume was really low. A box of crackers was on the coffee table. The sight of her was a huge relief. But only for a millisecond.

"What are you doing in here?" I asked.

"I'm sorry . . . your note said your parents wouldn't be back until four thirty or five, so I thought it was okay. I'm trying to find the news. You know, to see if I'm in it. Do you think I'm old news by now?"

"No. And you have to be careful. What if I had been wrong and my mom came home early? I mean, you don't want to get caught."

She nodded. "I don't want you to get caught, either."

"I'd get in big trouble for this," I said.

"I know. But hiding is boring."

"I have a bunch of books you can read," I told her. "And Joss is coming over." I explained about our cat sweater project.

"Okay." Charlotte shut the TV off. "I better head back to closet-ville."

I grabbed the box of crackers. "Keep these in case you need a snack when the coast isn't clear."

"Sure. And is it okay that I ate some of that lasagna in the fridge? I didn't leave any dirty dishes behind or anything."

"That's fine," I said.

Once Charlotte was back inside my closet, I quickly took the dog out to pee. I felt guilty because I usually would have walked him, but then I would have felt guilty about leaving Charlotte again.

When Waffles and I got back to my bedroom, Charlotte was standing by my desk holding a photo of my parents and me smiling outside of our diner. She held it a bit closer to her face before she set it down. She sighed.

"What's wrong?" I asked.

She turned around to face me. "Oh, how about pretty much everything?" She plopped back down inside the closet and pulled her knees to her chest. She wrapped her pale arms around her legs and dropped her head. I saw a tear slide off her face and hit the floor.

"Hey," I said, kneeling by her.

"Everything is wrong," she said again. Charlotte lifted her head up and wiped her nose. A part of me wanted to tell her to just go home. I thought about her parents and my own parents and how out of their minds with sadness they would be if I ever ran away. Especially if they had no idea if I was even okay. But she was my lucky charm.

"Living in someone's closet is hard," she said. Then she quickly added, "I mean, I'm thankful that you're letting me stay here, I am, really. But I don't like having to be here, you know? I really miss the twins. I want to go home."

"You want to leave?" I asked. I tried to make my words sound the opposite of what I was feeling in that second: borderline panicked.

"I was so mad when I left on Friday that I didn't ever want to go home," Charlotte said. "But now . . ."

"Now, what?" I asked her.

She lifted her head and reached for the croissant I offered her. "Now, even if I wanted to . . . I'm . . . I'm not sure if I can ever go home."

"I'm confused," I said.

She took a small bite. After she swallowed, she said, "I think I might have burned that house down."

CHAPTER
11

My mouth opened up so wide I could have probably parked the Enterprise inside it.

"But, I'm not positive," Charlotte said.

"Positive about what?" Joss asked, barging into my room with her knitting bag slung over her shoulder. "You guys should keep it down. What if I was Lizzy's mom? I could hear you in the hall." Fudge and Smoky trotted in before Joss kicked her leg behind her and gave my bedroom door a gentle boot. It slammed shut.

I looked at Charlotte. Was she going to say something? Or was I supposed to?

"I . . . I was worried that . . ." Charlotte looked at me and stopped talking.

"What? Tell me! What?" Joss looked at me. Waffles bumped up against Joss, asking for a scratch.

"I ran away the day before you found me. I left Friday right when I finished school. By the time I found the empty apartment, it was dark outside. It was freezing cold in there. And I tried to light some dried leaves in the fireplace. I found some matches under the sink."

"You burned the house down!" Joss practically screeched.

"She couldn't have," I said, thinking about when Joss and I had climbed through the window to look for the cat. "I mean . . . when exactly did you light the fire? Because when we got there the next morning we didn't see or smell anything burning in the fire-place—right, Joss?

"I didn't do a great job trying to start one. I couldn't get a match to light. They were kind of wet. But I tried. After the third try, I realized that if I did light a fire, someone might see the smoke coming out of the chimney and find me. So I just gave up."

"Well then, that couldn't have caused a house to catch on fire," I said. "Could it?"

"Maybe I didn't realize that I sparked something . . . and then it smoldered . . . and maybe a leaf caught on fire . . . or something . . ."

"Like, so many hours later?" I asked. "Is that possible?"

All three of us shrugged at the same time.

"I have no clue," Joss said. "But that doesn't sound very possible to me."

"Especially if you didn't even light the match," I added.

"But it's not *impossible,* either, right?" Charlotte asked.

"I think it had to be some other thing that caused it," I said.

"Even if by some crazy way you did spark something, it was just an accident," Joss pointed out.

"But I shouldn't have been in there in the first place. I'm a runaway and . . . an intruder . . . and now maybe a fire starter."

"Don't put it like that," Joss said, "it sounds even worse."

Charlotte's eyes filled up. "And there's something else . . ."

What else could there be? I wanted to shout.

"You know how you asked why I came to East Thumb? Well, it's true I only had twelve dollars for the bus, but I also knew I'd have a place to hide. I knew that apartment house was empty."

"How did you know?"

"The guy that owns it is a client of my mom's. I saw some paperwork about it on her desk."

"Client?" I asked.

"She's a lawyer. She helps people who go broke and can't pay their bills."

"So you may have burned down this broke guy's house?" I tried asking in such a gentle way it didn't even sound like my voice.

"*Accidently* burned down," Joss said. "Don't forget that part." She reached into the closet and patted Charlotte's shoulder. "I mean, he obviously wasn't living in it anymore," she added.

"Wait!" I said, remembering what my mom had told me that morning about desperate people doing desperate things. I explained about the insurance money. "Maybe your mom's client burned down his own house!" Especially if Bibi was right about the fire being set on purpose.

"Did you see anyone?" Joss asked.

"How could she? She was in the closet!" I said.

But Charlotte was shaking her head no. "And I definitely would have heard if someone had come in the house. I heard you two talking on the front porch. Why do you think I went to hide in the closet?"

"Oh," Joss and I said together.

"Maybe he started the fire from the outside of the house?"

"In broad daylight?" Charlotte asked.

"That would be dumb," I said. "Not that burning your own house down isn't dumb in the first place. And illegal!" I added, quoting my mom. "But still, I think it's just a major freaky coincidence that you tried to light a fire and then the house burned down."

None of us said anything because it was major freaky.

"That is a pretty awful coincidence," Joss finally said.

Charlotte's lip quivered. "It probably was me. See why I can't go home?" she whispered. She leaned her head against the closet wall and shut her eyes. "I'm going to be in so much trouble." A tear slid down her cheek.

"Well, you can stay here as long as you want. As long as you need to," I said. "Until we know what really happened with the fire." My heart bloomed like a bouquet of flowers inside my chest at the thought of my good luck charm possibly staying until the baby was born. But I tried to squeeze out that sunny scenario. I slammed that door closed on my brain. It wasn't nice to be happy about something that was the cause of someone else's unhappiness.

"Don't worry," Joss said. Then she looked at me. I could tell she couldn't think of something else to say to make Charlotte feel better and wanted my help.

I picked up Charlotte's hand. "Did you draw this, or is it one of those transfer tattoos? It looks so perfect," I said.

"I made it," she said. She took a green marker out of her bag. "With this. You want one?" she asked, pulling off the top. It was the kind of ink that didn't rub off. The kind Mom used to write my name on the inside of the clothes I took to school for gym and to summer camp. Permanent ink. *Another sign?* That the luck Charlotte would bring was permanent, too?

"Pick a design," she said, handing Joss her journal—the one I had seen in Dad's truck.

"Wow. You're amazing!" Joss said when she opened it up. She

flipped through the pages. "Look at this." She held Charlotte's journal up for me to see.

"I can draw whatever you want," Charlotte said.

I looked up to see animals and faces and bugs and flowers. Some were just little pictures, but some were whole scenes with so much color and detail I didn't know where to look first. It was like everything beautiful in the world in every color on the pages. "Wow," I said. "This is really, really good. You're so talented. Do you want to be an artist when you grow up?"

"You don't have to be a grown-up to be an artist," Charlotte said.

"True," I told her.

"Can you do a tiger in a tree like the one you drew here?" Joss pointed to a page in the journal.

"Of course," Charlotte said.

Joss rolled up her sleeve and held out her arm.

"I'll have the same as you," I said to Charlotte.

"That's so boring," Joss said. "No offense, Charlotte," she added. "It's just that her art is unbelievable. Look what you have for options!" she said to me.

But I didn't care about options. I could only think about how extra lucky it had to be for this good luck girl to personally decorate my hand with my own four-leaf clover.

CHAPTER 12

WHEN CHARLOTTE FINISHED OUR TATTOOS, JOSS pulled out her knitting stuff.

"Knitting 101. Ready?"

"Whoa," I said, "those are weird looking. And kind of fat."

"They're circular needles. And the thicker the yarn, the fatter the needles, so . . ." Joss handed them to us. "It will be much faster and easier to knit the sweaters in a tube shape. Plus, you only need to learn the knit stitch and not the purl."

"You're teaching me, too?" Charlotte said.

"Of course! The more the merrier." We rummaged through the bags of yarn. I chose a green ball, the color of a celery stick, to match Smoky's eyes.

"Let's see, Smoky," I said, holding the yarn by his face. Charlotte and Joss each chose different shades of purple.

"FYI," I said, "to reach our goal of raising five hundred dollars for the shelter, we have to sell about fifty sweaters."

"That's a lot," Charlotte said.

"It's seventeen sweaters each. Well, sixteen and two thirds technically, but I rounded up for obvious reasons. If we knit one, sometimes two a day," I said, "we might be able to have them done in about two weeks."

"That doesn't sound bad," Joss said.

"Actually, you could probably finish your seventeen in just a few days," I told Charlotte.

Charlotte looked down at the floor. I waited for her to say something like, I won't be here that long. But she didn't. She just said, "Probably."

"Okay, watch," Joss said to us. "First, let's cast on." She unrolled some yarn from her ball. Right away Fudge and Smoky pounced at the strand. "Hey!" Joss said. "Knock it off, you two." Each time any of us unraveled yarn, Fudge and Smoky went nuts at it.

"Sorry, boys," I said, tucking a cat under each of my arms and locking them out of my room. "Where were we?" I picked my needles back up.

"Wrap the yarn like this and make a loop. That's just a slip knot," Joss said. She watched to make sure we did it right. "We need to cast on forty-eight stitches. I'll show you how. Then, we'll add a marker."

"What's a marker?" I asked.

"This." Joss reached into her bag and pulled out three little rings. Each had a red knitted rose hanging from it. "We'll slide one of these onto our needles. It marks your spot so you'll be able to tell when a round ends and begins."

"Sounds good to me," Charlotte said. "But what's a round?"

"It's basically like a row, but since we're using circular needles, it's called a round."

Even with my previous, though pretty awful history with knitting, I still wasn't sure what I was doing. I watched Joss closely. I noticed Charlotte, who had never knit before in her life, was catching on fast. "You're good," I said to her.

She laughed. "I haven't really done much yet."

"Well, you don't look confused. That's a good sign for a rookie."

"Thanks," she said.

After some more instruction and practice, we were all knitting away. Joss checked regularly to make sure we weren't messing up and helped us when we did. "Stop when you've knit twenty rounds. I'll show you how to do the holes for legs. Or I'll take over and you can start a new sweater," she told us. "I've got plenty of extra needles."

"Okay," we answered at the same time.

We didn't talk much since we were busy concentrating. But

this seemed way easier than knitting for a human. There weren't many knitwear options for cats. I didn't have to master any of the tricky stuff, like thumbs or sleeves or pockets, which would have totally thrown me off my game.

When I was halfway through my first sweater, I got up to turn on my bedroom lights. By the time Charlotte and I each had a finished product and Joss was a quarter way through her second, the sun had disappeared completely.

Joss's phone lit up. "Whoa, I have to leave. It's almost five o'clock. My dad is here to get me," she said, gathering her yarn. "You guys seem to have the hang of it. Text if you need help." She opened the door just as Mom was about to knock.

I kicked my closet door shut so Charlotte was out of sight.

"Hello there, sweeties!" Mom said. Fudge strolled in with her. Waffles, who'd been asleep on my bed, picked his head up, then bounced over to my mother for a greeting.

"Hello. And good-bye!" Joss said. She looked back over her shoulder at me. Her eyes were like two silver dollar pancakes. She glanced my mother's way to make sure she wasn't watching before she mouthed *OMG* to me.

"Bye, Joss," Mom said. Then to me, "How was your day? Did you get what you needed in Portland?"

"Yes. We got great stuff." I gathered some of the yarn to show her.

Fudge went straight to my closet door and rubbed against it. Waffles sniffed at the floor in front of it.

"You know I've noticed the two of them have been spending a lot of extra time in your room lately."

"You have?" *What else was she starting to notice?* My throw pillows and my afghan missing from my bed? The junk that used to be on the floor of the closet piled on my desk?

"Yes, haven't you?" she asked me. "Waffles usually sleeps in our bedroom at night. I think maybe Fudge and Waffles are looking for more of your attention since Smoky moved in." She looked at me. Was she waiting for an explanation?

"Maybe," I said. I picked up Fudge and sat with him on my bed, distracting him with a piece of yarn. Waffles whined at the closet door.

"Listen to Waffles. He sounds jealous of the attention you're giving to Fudge, too. What's the matter, silly poodle? You feeling insecure with a new cat in the house?" Mom scratched his head, and Waffle's tail swished against the floor.

I took a deep breath because it felt hard to breathe.

"Anyway," Mom said, "did you eat the rest of the lasagna?"

"Um . . . I can't remember."

"How can you not remember? Either you ate it or you didn't."

Charlotte. "Oh, that's right, I did. Sorry," I said.

"Not to worry. I'll figure something else out. I'll call you when it's ready. By the way, your favorite dad brought you cookie dough ice cream for dessert."

"Yum!" I said, before my mom left and shut the door.

"You're so lucky you have a nice dad," Charlotte said in the saddest voice, from inside the closet.

She was right. I didn't need any luck from her for that.

"My dad used to be nice. But now he doesn't really care about any of us anymore," Charlotte continued.

I opened my closet. Waffles bounced on Charlotte, licking her face. "Your dad does care," I told her. But how did I really know that was true? I had never even met him before. I just couldn't imagine my dad not caring.

"Well, he should act like he cares." She nuzzled against Waffles. "I mean, I can't picture my dad not living with us anymore. But I guess he can."

A little while later when I sat down at the kitchen table, I didn't feel much like eating my dinner, never mind my favorite ice cream. Charlotte's sadness had my brain in a ball of spaghetti, all tangled up again with a batch of new worries.

I thought about her and her broken family. I wondered about runaway daughters and dads. I didn't believe that Charlotte's father was leaving because he no longer loved her and her brother and sister, but she totally believed it. And with Charlotte gone, her mom and the twins had *two* reasons to feel heartbroken. I felt sad for them. Because I knew how much it hurt to miss someone you loved. Even if they never meant to leave you behind.

CHAPTER
13

THE NEXT MORNING, SID SHOWED UP AT OUR apartment with a paper bag. Since I was taking Smoky with me to school, Dad didn't want me stopping into the diner with a cat to pick up the breakfast he was making for Elle, Joss, and me.

"Here you go, Lizzy," Sid said when I opened the door. "Bon appétit. And good luck with your cat sweater thing." He turned and headed back down the stairs.

"Thank you," I called after him. I unrolled the top of the paper sack. The bag was warm, and the smell of egg and cheese drifted up my nose and made me feel hungrier than I already was. The extra breakfast sandwich I had Dad make for "another friend" was in there, too. I brought it back to my room for Charlotte, who was still asleep. For a split second, I thought how lucky she was not to have to get up and go to school. Then I remembered why she was here.

I propped the sandwich against the closet wall so she (a) couldn't miss it and (b) wouldn't roll over and squish it.

In the kitchen, Smoky meowed. I bent down and poked my finger between the metal bars of the cat carrier and tickled his cheek. He sniffed my hand.

"It's okay, sweetie. You're only in here for a little bit. You get to come to school with me, you lucky boy." The cat meowed again, and I felt a jolt of guilt that he was locked up. While I waited for my ride, I sat on the floor next to him and ate my breakfast, treating him to small little bits of egg and cheese.

● ● ●

The radio in Elle's car blasted a bunch of metal noise.

"Hey, Smoky, buckle up," Joss said, turning down the music.

"Hello, handsome," Elle said to him.

"Breakfast, anyone?" I dropped the two sandwiches into the front seat as we drove off.

"Thanks," they said.

"Elle, look," I held my cat sweater up. "This is the one we're going to model on him." Smoky let out a meow, and we laughed at his perfect timing. He sniffed at the door to his cage, and I patted his velvety nose with my finger. "You can't wait, can you?" I asked him.

Joss twisted herself around as much as her seat belt allowed her to. She pulled a yellow sweater out of her backpack and held it up. "I knit another one last night. This is for Ms. Santorelli's cat. She said she wanted a bright color."

"Nice," I said.

Joss stuffed the sweater back in her bag and unwrapped her sandwich. She took a huge bite. "This is so good," she mumbled with her mouth full.

A few minutes later, Elle pulled into the school drop-off lot and stopped. "See ya," she said, as Joss and I slid out of the car. "Good luck, Smoky."

We thanked her for the ride, and she drove off.

"We're lucky we got permission to bring him in," Joss said.

That was true.

East Thumb had only two schools: Central Elementary, K through sixth; and Central High, seventh through twelfth. Most sixth graders from bigger towns had a different teacher for every subject, but at Central Elementary, except for art, gym, and computer, we had one teacher for all the subjects. *And* we had a principal that was cool enough to allow a cat to visit.

"Do you think Smoky needs to wear a visitor's badge?" I asked.

Joss laughed.

● ● ●

In class, everyone wanted to see the cat.

"Give him some space, please! He's not a circus act." I pulled the carrier behind my knees to give Smoky some privacy.

"Quit making him nervous," Joss said to everyone.

"Where's the sweater?" Cooper asked. "How come she's not wearing one?"

"It's a he," I said. "And he's not wearing it yet because we're going to demonstrate how to put one on your cat."

"I don't have a cat," Zoe said.

"I know you don't. But you can always get a sweater for someone else's cat. Or better, adopt a cat for yourself. They have plenty at the Lodge," I said.

"My mom's allergic," she told me.

I shrugged.

"But I'll get one for my cousin's cat," Zoe said.

"Thank you," I said.

"Ah! Our little guest of honor has arrived." Ms. Santorelli knelt down and smiled into the carrier. Her dangling bead earrings, that she made herself, swung slightly, and the glasses that she was always looking for were propped on the top of her head, like a headband in her awesome chin-length hair.

"I love this idea," she said to Joss and me. She had already told us that our cat sweater fund-raiser for the Lodge was a perfect example of kindness. Because of us, she had created a giant "Heart the World" idea board in our classroom. She wanted the board to inspire the rest of the class to come up with their own ideas on how they could "spread around love and compassion to others."

She was participating, too. She was going to make and sell "Beads for Bread" bracelets and donate the profits to the East Thumb food pantry.

"Where's your cat sweater poster for the board?" she asked us. "I want it up as inspiration. Let's see in the next few days if we can fill up our board with some other great ideas!" she hollered out to the class.

"We're still working on the poster," I told her. "I'll bring it in tomorrow." With all the knitting and stuff with Charlotte, I hadn't had time to make one.

"You two, wait right over there," she said to Joss and me as she pointed to the front of the classroom. "After morning announcements, you'll tell us all about the wonderful way you are helping out the animal shelter and sending love into the universe." She walked to her messy desk just as the morning bell rang. Everyone but us sat down.

The vice principal droned on over the PA system about what time the science club would meet, and what was on Monday's lunch menu. He recapped Friday night's high school football win, which most of us had seen firsthand. I yawned.

"Has there been any more news about the fire? Like, who set it?" Joss whispered to me.

"I haven't heard anything."

Ms. Santorelli looked over at us and put her fingers to her lips.

When the announcements ended, Ms. Santorelli said, "All right, take it away, girls."

Joss spoke first. "For the past year, Lizzy and I have been spending time at the Community Lodge for Cats & Dogs helping out. We mostly do stuff like play with the cats, and fold laundry."

"Laundry?" Zoe asked.

"Yes. Stuff needs to be washed there all the time," I said. "Towels, blankets . . . cats love snuggling in whatever."

"So," Joss continued, "one time when we were there helping out, we saw a sign for the Tails and Trails 5K run. The race raises money for the Lodge. Lizzy and I started brainstorming about other ways to help. That's when we came up with our plan to knit and sell cat sweaters."

"The shelter gets lots of donations, but they still need money to pay for food and medical care for the animals," I explained to the class. "And the funds will help the dogs, too."

Zoe shouted out, "Yay!" because she's way more of a dog person, with her mom's cat allergies and her four beagles.

Joss held up the sweater. "Introducing Cozy Cat sweaters. I made this!" she announced. The class clapped. "Lizzy made one, too. And she brought in Smoky, so we can show you how easy it is to put one on your cat."

"It's like wearing a little blanket," I said. "And FYI, these sweaters are just ten dollars, or two for eighteen."

"Are they just for shelter cats?" Cooper asked.

"Any cat would love one," I said, sounding like an ad on TV. "But if you don't have your own cat at home, you can buy one for a shelter cat."

"And you get a free one of these with your sweater order." Joss held up a decal and made sure everyone got a close look at it.

"Shelter cats don't even go outside. Why do they need a sweater?" Cooper asked.

"Lots of cats don't go outside. And the shelter has a screened-in play area for the cats, so technically they do spend time outdoors." Joss sounded irritated that Cooper wasn't getting it. I elbowed her to stay cool.

"Anyway," I said, "the sweaters aren't only to keep the cats warm. They're pretty lightweight."

Joss held one up and pulled at the knitting. "The main reason for the sweater is they keep the cat feeling cozy. Like they're wearing a cozy little blanket. Get it? Cozy Cat sweaters?"

Joss modeled the sweater over her arm while I squeezed the safety latch on the carrier.

"Smoky will show you how snuggly they are," I said. The little door swung open, but Smoky was way back inside, crouched up against the rear grill. "Come on, sweetie," I cooed. "It's okay. You're okay." I reached in and drummed my fingers on the floor of the cage. Smoky stretched his neck forward and sniffed at my hand. He slowly crept closer to the front. "Good boy." I pulled him out and up, holding him against my chest and patting the top of his head.

"Now watch how easy it is to put one on," Joss announced, gently stretching open the neck of the sweater. Before she could get two steps closer to me, Smoky catapulted off my shoulder and landed on the teacher's desk. I felt a sharp sting by my collarbone from his claws. I saw Ms. Santorelli's eyeballs peek over the top of her eyeglass frames. Smoky sprang to the floor, and papers and pens rained down behind him.

The class exploded into laughter while Joss and I scrambled to catch my cat.

"I don't think he likes sweaters," someone yelled out.

"I'll help you get him," someone else offered.

"Me too," Cooper said, right before Smoky bolted out the classroom door.

CHAPTER
14

"NOT TOO SWIFT OF ME TO LEAVE THAT DOOR open," I heard Ms. Santorelli say as I raced down the hall after the cat.

"Smoky! Stop!" I yelled. He looked at me and waited. He arched his back and pressed himself against the wall. Cooper and Zoe came flying out of the classroom, and with the noise and commotion, Smoky shot off again.

"Come on," I said to Joss. We turned the corner at the end of the hallway and almost smacked into Mr. Sols, the custodian.

"Whose cat is that?" he asked. Smoky was a few feet behind him.

"Mine," I said, dodging around him. The cat seemed to be considering which way to run next. I slowed down and took small, soft steps toward him. When I was almost close enough to scoop him up, he shot off into the computer classroom.

"I'll go get his carrier," Joss said. I followed my cat into the room, which thankfully was empty, and quickly shut the door behind me. Luckily, there were no computer classes first thing on Mondays.

Smoky sat down on the opposite side of the room. He rubbed his head against the metal heating vent in the wall.

"It's okay. I'm sorry you got scared," I told him. I didn't dare to move closer, so I lowered myself to the floor. I would wait until he was relaxed enough to come to me. "You are a good boy."

I wished Joss would hurry with the carrier. Maybe now Smoky couldn't wait to get back inside of it. While I made little kissing noises, trying to get him to move closer to me, I noticed a small hole next to the vent. I wondered if he could fit into such a little space. Smoky noticed the hole, too, and seemed to wonder the exact same thing. He sniffed at the edges, then he peeked inside.

"No!" I shouted, startling him. He jerked his head up. His ears twitched. Then he went right back to sniffing at it again. I rushed over to him, but before I could grab him, he disappeared inside the wall. I dropped to my knees and peered inside. I couldn't see a thing except a whole bunch of pitch-black. "Smoky!"

I heard the door open and close softly. "He discover that hole there, did he?" Mr. Sols asked.

I couldn't answer, my throat was so tight.

"Uh-huh," Mr. Sols answered his own question. "Cats are a curious bunch, aren't they?"

The hole started just a couple of inches above the floor. The opening was only about the size of a softball. But Smoky was a skinny cat. A skinny, missing cat.

Joss came in with the carrier.

"No way!" she said, spotting the hole.

"I'll stay and see if the cat comes out," Mr. Sols told us. "You two, go get some food that we can entice him with."

• • •

"He's hiding in a wall!" Joss announced when we got back to the classroom.

"Probably because he doesn't want to wear a dumb sweater," Cooper said.

"Cooper!" Zoe yelled at him.

"I better notify the principal and let her know there's a missing cat," Ms. Santorelli said.

"Is Lizzy in trouble?" Zoe asked.

"Of course not. Not at all. And don't worry, Lizzy," Ms. Santorelli said as she put her arm around my shoulders. "He'll come out." Then she smiled at me just like Elle had when she had asked about the baby. It was a little too wide, and she was not saying, but was probably thinking, *hopefully*.

"He needs to come out now," I said. My voice sounded shaky.

"The classroom will be full of students soon. He'll be scared."

"Try not to panic, sweetie," Ms. Santorelli said. "Worst-case scenario, he'll wait until the coast is clear. He won't stay in there forever."

"I need to tell my mom. I told her to come get Smoky by nine thirty. I have to tell her he's gone." I pulled out my phone and texted her the bad news.

"Don't worry, Lizzy," said Joss. "He's probably just having fun. Remember how he likes to jump in and out of closets?"

"That's weird," Cooper said. "Why does he do that?"

"Because he does, okay?" Joss said, splaying her hands out at him. "What's it to you?"

"We need food," I said. "He'll come out to eat."

"I've got a turkey sandwich," Zoe said. "I can buy lunch if someone lends me money."

"You kids, keep your lunches. I brought a turkey sandwich today, too," Ms. Santorelli said. "We'll put some of the meat on a plate and leave it in the computer room."

"Maybe he's too nervous to be hungry," Cooper was saying. "What if he doesn't come out? What if he *can't* get out?"

"He just finished being a lost cat," I said. I blinked fast so the tears I felt pooling wouldn't spill out.

"Let's leave the food and see what happens," my teacher said.

Sandwich specials of the every-other-day-or-so were always

popping into my head at random times. But there was nothing random about where my brain was going with this one. Right smack in the middle of two tons of worry, it was all about Smoky. Smoked Black Forest ham, a ring of pineapple, swiss cheese on a dark rye bagel. What else would I call it but the Black Hole?

• • •

By lunch, I had checked the computer room three more times. Mrs. Potter, the computer teacher, was usually a crab cake on the best of days. But she must have felt sorry for me, or maybe my cat. She was nice about letting me come in to check the hole, even though my barging into her room disrupted her classes.

"He hasn't come out yet," she told me each time. And I could see that the turkey was still on the plate. I had no appetite, either.

In spite of everything, there was a steady stream of kids coming over to our lunch table to order Cozy Cat sweaters.

"Sympathy buys," Joss whispered in my ear. "But we'll take it."

I could hear the conversations happening around me, but my mind was far, far away. Behind the walls of the school. What was he doing in there? Was there enough air? What about electrical wires? I grabbed the edge of the lunch table. *What if he chewed on one?*

Someone across from me was asking about monogramming.

What's that? Joss wanted to know.

Initials, someone explained.

This isn't L.L.Bean! I heard her answer.

I felt like a complete fraud selling the sweaters now. I was supposed to be helping animals, not setting them up to run away again. What sign had I missed to warn me that bringing a cat to school was a stupid idea? I should have been more focused. Because the signs were out there. I had to pay better attention. Terrible things happened when I didn't. What if Smoky was stuck forever? What if he died in there?

When I noticed Mr. Sols standing by our table, my brain still felt like it was bubble-wrapped. Joss shook my arm, and I snapped to attention.

"He's out?" I said, jumping up from my seat. "Where is he?" I smiled at Mr. Sols. The lunch table cheered.

"Well, no," Mr. Sols said. "But when the classroom cleared, he must have come out to eat. The plate is licked clean. Then he went back inside the wall."

My heart wilted. "Didn't Mrs. Potter try to catch him?"

"Apparently, she was in the restroom when it happened," he said.

"But we know now he can find his way out! That's great news, Lizzy," Joss said.

There were lots of times when I wished I spoke "cat," and this was one of them. Like when a shelter cat was sick and couldn't be let out of its cage to play with the other cats. Usually, the sick cat would cry, and I'd try to explain that it wasn't because they weren't as loved. It was just because they were contagious. But cats don't understand stuff like spreadable germs.

So, even though I spoke into the hole and explained to Smoky that it was safe to come out, he wouldn't. Because I can't speak cat and he can't understand human. Except when I hug him and kiss the top of his head. He can understand that. But I couldn't do that, because by the end of the day, he still hadn't come out.

CHAPTER
15

Joss convinced me to head home rather than stay after school.

"You know how cats are. They don't listen on purpose. He'll be out tomorrow. Plus, you'll feel better after ice cream." We hustled across the walkway to our school bus.

I nodded. I knew what she meant about cats not listening. I had texted my mom an update and left Smoky a pile of chicken salad from one half of my uneaten sandwich. I saved the rest for Charlotte.

"You think Charlotte will feel as bad as I do about Smoky? She loves him, too. I hope she isn't mad at me." I grabbed Joss's arm. "What if she gets so mad, she leaves?" If having Charlotte in my house was supposed to bring me good luck, what horrible thing was waiting to happen if she left? My stomach felt like it was full of broken glass.

"I bet you anything he'll be waiting for you when we go in tomorrow," Joss said for the second time.

The door flaps closed, and the bus lurched forward. On the ride home, I hoped like crazy Smoky would be waiting for me tomorrow. If he wasn't, I wondered if Charlotte wouldn't be waiting for me *after* school tomorrow, either.

• • •

It was just a few minutes past three thirty when we got to the diner, which was already closed for the day. Bibi pulled the door open when we knocked.

"Good afternoon, sugar cookies," she said. She had her coat on like she was ready to leave. But she shut the door behind us, relocked it, and went into the kitchen to chat with Sid.

Joss and I plunked down at the counter.

"You know what I think?"

"What?" Joss asked.

I swiveled my seat in her direction so our knees touched. "At first, I thought I missed a sign that a cat school visit was a bad idea. But now I realize that Smoky disappearing into the wall *was* the sign."

"Of what?" Joss sighed and rolled her eyes, but I didn't care.

"A sign that we should let Charlotte's parents know that she's okay," I whispered.

"Really?"

"When Smoky disappeared, I felt sick to my stomach. But once I knew he could find his way out, and that he was okay, I felt better. We have to try to make her parents feel better."

"How do we do that?"

"We could send an anonymous letter. Or an e-mail would be much faster. We'd let them know that she's safe," I said softly.

"What if the e-mail gets traced back to us? We could get in lots of trouble for hiding someone. Especially if the police are looking for her. Besides, if we do that behind Charlotte's back, it would be kind of like us being tattletales."

I hadn't thought about that. Bibi walked over holding a to-go container.

Sid yelled to us from behind the griddle. "Hey, girls. Ice cream?"

"For sure, thanks," Joss said.

"Two cookie doughs. One with sprinkles, one with hot fudge," he said to us.

"Thanks, Sid," I told him. He popped his head through the space above the griddle. I gave him a thumbs-up. And he gave me two thumbs-up back and a smile.

Bibi was still standing by me, and she placed her hand on my shoulder. "Hey, sugar. I'm not going to beat around the bush here. Your dad was not feeling well today," she told me. "But he's okay, now. I promise." She moved her hand to my head and patted my hair.

I looked around me. What a dope I was to not even notice he wasn't here. I had figured Dad was in the back office where he often was when the diner closed. "Where is he?" I asked.

"He's at home."

"Dad never, ever misses work," I said.

"I know. But don't be worried, he's fine," Bibi said, sliding the to-go container in front of me. "Sid made chicken soup for you to bring home to him." I had barely had the chance to let worry sink in. But the way she looked at me, with her head tilted to one side and her eyes all sweet and a little sad, I started to panic.

"What's wrong with my dad?" I jumped off the stool. I felt my throat tighten up. What sign had I missed where I didn't see this coming?

"He was feeling . . . uncomfortable . . . during the breakfast rush."

"What kind of uncomfortable?" Joss asked, before I could get the words out.

"He said his chest hurt. He did scare us. But luck was with us, and there was a doctor in the diner this morning."

I looked at Joss. "That was lucky," I said.

"It wasn't very lucky that he wasn't feeling well in the first place," Joss pointed out.

"But, sugar, he's good as gold now," she quickly added. "Your mom took him to the ER earlier and everything was fine."

"What?" I hollered. "The *emergency* room?"

"Turned out to be nothing serious," Sid yelled from the kitchen. "Not his heart. Just his heartburn flaring up again."

"That's right," Bibi tried to assure me. "They ran all the right tests, and he feels much better. He even wanted to come back in to work. But your mother said no. We convinced him to take the rest of the day off."

"Can we get those ice creams to go?" Joss asked Sid.

"Sorry. I can't think of ice cream right now," I said. I grabbed the soup, my bag, and my coat.

Joss caught up with me as I was running up the stairs to the apartment.

"Dad!" I yelled as I burst inside. He was sitting at the kitchen table with a pile of paperwork.

"Hey, honey. Shhhhhh . . . Mom is napping. I saw the texts you sent her. Sorry about your bad day," he said to me. "Smoky will be back. He's just being a cat."

"My bad day? Are you okay?" I put the soup down, dropped my stuff on the floor, and gave him a hug.

"I'm fine. I'm fine."

"But Sid said you thought you were having a heart attack!"

Dad shook his head no. "It wasn't. It was nothing like that.

By the way, did Sid tell you that your smokestack sandwich was a hit?"

"Dad, are you really okay?" He didn't look any different than he usually did, which made me relax a bit.

"It was just heartburn. That's all. Now come on. Sit down and let's talk sandwiches."

Dad pulled out the chair next to him and patted the seat.

"Fine," I said. I sat down. Joss sat, too, and pushed my cup of ice cream in front of me.

I told him about the Black Hole sandwich. "But I thought of another one for later this week, too. The Early Riser."

"How did you come up with it?" he asked me.

"Ever hear the saying, 'Early to bed, early to rise makes a man healthy, wealthy, and wise'?"

"You know Ben Franklin?" Joss asked my dad.

"Not personally, but I've heard of him." Dad winked at me.

"We're reading about him at school. That thing he said made me think of a breakfast sandwich. A turned-up version of our roll-up: egg, cheese, and ham or bacon, but for the special we'll serve it between two pieces of french toast! You like it?"

"It sounds phenomenal. You have the best ideas." He smiled at me.

"Speaking of ideas . . . you know our cat sweater sale at the diner we're having on Saturday?" I asked.

"I'm listening." He tucked his pen behind his ear. "You're not going to ask me to offer a free meal to anyone who orders a sweater, are you?"

"Hey, we didn't think of that," I said, "but no, that's not what I was going to ask you. We want to have some of the shelter cats around while we take cat sweater orders. It would definitely help to put a face to our cause."

"A cat face," Joss added.

"Diners and stray cats don't mix, girls," Dad said.

"But it's a *sidewalk* event. They won't come inside. It will be awesome. People will see the cats, order a sweater, and then go inside for a meal. It will be good for your business, too."

"Well." Dad swallowed back a burp and tapped at the middle of his chest. I gave him a worried look. But he shook his head and said, "Heartburn. Now, as far as your fund-raiser, it all sounds great. We'll make it work."

Joss held her fist out for me to bump. But before we touched knuckles, my brain threw itself into reverse. I had an awful thought. *Could* we make it work? Would it be great? Would any-one even show up to our event knowing that it was 100 percent because of *me* that my own cat had run away? How lame was it to think anyone would want to buy a Cozy Cat sweater if they thought that Smoky was holed up in a wall just so he wouldn't have to wear one?

My spaghetti brain was back. A big, sticky, knotted mess. I had better hurry up and get it untangled.

CHAPTER 16

AFTER JOSS LEFT, I WENT STRAIGHT TO MY ROOM
to see Charlotte.

"Hey," I said, closing my bedroom door.

"You didn't tell me your parents were coming home early!"
she said. She swung the closet door open and stretched out
her legs. Fudge hopped off her lap and trotted over to see me. I
kneeled down to scratch his head. I should have used him instead
of Smoky for the demonstration.

"I didn't know," I said, feeling annoyed. "Remember yesterday
when you were watching TV in the living room? I told you to be
careful? I can't help if they decide to leave work early. I can't control everything." Those words surprised me when I heard them
come out of my mouth. Joss was always saying, *you can't control
everything*, when she brushed off my signs.

"I finished the crackers." Charlotte held up the box and shook it. "It's like torture smelling diner food every second. I'm practically drooling on myself." She sounded cranky, too. I couldn't really blame her, being crammed in a tiny closet and hungry. But I had had a bad day, too.

I scooted closer to her and handed her the half sandwich I had saved and the rest of my ice cream.

"Thanks," she said. Charlotte pushed the sandwich into her mouth, taking a huge bite. She watched me while she chewed, and I looked away. "What's wrong?" she asked, after she swallowed.

"Lots," I said.

"Does it have to do with why your parents were home early?"

"My dad wasn't feeling well." Then I explained what happened and how he had to go to the hospital.

"I'm sorry, Lizzy. I didn't know," Charlotte said. "He's okay now, right?"

"I think so. And I'm sorry, too, if I sounded a little nasty, but . . . I've had a really crummy day."

Charlotte nodded. "How did it go with Smoky?" she asked.

"It didn't go well." Fudge stepped onto my lap.

"What happened? He didn't cooperate?"

"No, he didn't . . . I mean, it's bad . . ." I swallowed hard, holding back the tears that had been trying to spill out all day.

"What's bad?" Charlotte asked. She stopped chewing.

I sucked in a huge gulp of air and let it out in slow motion before I told her. "Smoky's missing."

"What do you mean missing? Where'd he go?"

"He's in a hole in a wall," I explained. I looked away from her. It sounded as bad as it was. I bit my lower lip to stop it from quivering.

"What happened?"

I explained how the cat had gotten spooked and run. "I really didn't think he'd do that. I mean, of course I didn't think that, because then I never would have brought him to school." My throat tightened, and I had to stop talking. When I could speak again, I added, "I'm really sorry. I know he's like your cat, too. I feel awful he's inside that hole."

Charlotte nodded. "I guess hiding out in a hole in the wall isn't the worst thing. The reason for hiding is much worse. I should know, right?"

"Yeah" was the only thing I could think of to say, because it was totally true. I knew she was talking about her parents. But it was true for Smoky, too. He must have been scared to death. I saw a tear slide down her face. And I let mine go, too.

Charlotte reached out of the closet and wiped my cheek with the back of her hand. She sniffed and wiped her eyes. "But I also know he can't hide forever," Charlotte said. "I mean, he probably won't want to. Hiding out gets pretty boring."

Cats sort of like being bored, I thought, but decided not to point out.

"I don't know what Smoky is doing in his hole in the wall," Charlotte continued, "but besides thinking about eating, I did some knitting." She held up a finished cat sweater and a second that was about halfway done.

"Those are great! Even the leg holes, wow." I wasn't sure I'd be able to do leg holes without Joss's help. But I guess Charlotte could show me. She smiled a little bit, and I smiled back at her.

Charlotte reached to the side of the closet. "And I made these." She held up a colorful poster. There was a gray cat wearing a sweater in the middle of it. Smoky. He was floating above Earth, and there were other planets and stars and a yellow moon around him. To spell out "Heart the World," she had drawn a giant red heart in front of the words "the world." It seemed to float across the page like it was drifting in outer space. A second poster had a cat curled up in a puddle of yellow sunshine napping on a heart-shaped rug, and another cat stretched out over the back of a chair that was covered in hearts. All the cats were wearing Cozy Cat sweaters.

"These are awesome!" I told her.

"Thanks. Lots of little hearts make up that one big heart, see."

I hadn't noticed before, but I saw them all now. There must have been at least a hundred tiny red hearts, together, forming the shape of the one big heart. "Wow. That must have taken a long time," I said.

"Yup. Good thing I have lots of it to spare. You said you didn't have time to do it yesterday, so I thought I'd help you."

"Thank you." I studied the posters, and when I looked up, I saw that Charlotte was crying again.

"It's so weird, isn't it?" she asked, holding up the poster with all the little hearts. "Making this poster about love. And there's, like, none at all left in my family."

"Don't say that. No matter what, your parents still love you," I said.

"Not enough to keep us a family, though, right? What problem could be so big that you would leave your own family?"

"You left yours," I said.

Charlotte wiped at her nose. "Because we aren't going to be a family anymore. But when they finally see that . . . and my dad changes his mind . . . I mean . . . how would you feel if your dad told you he was going to leave?"

"It would stink. But I know my dad loves me no matter what."

"You're so lucky. No one in your family has ever left you."

But that wasn't true. I did know what it felt like to have someone leave my family. Not in the way her dad was leaving hers. But it still hurt.

I heard a knock at my bedroom door. Charlotte pulled in her

legs. I jumped up and practically fell against the closet door, closing her inside.

"Hi, lovely," Mom said, strolling into my room. "You okay?"

My heart pounded. *How much drama could one person take in a single day?*

"I'm sad," I said a little breathlessly.

Mom rolled her bottom lip into a frown and tipped her head to the side. Her way of saying, *I get it. I'm sorry.* "I know it seems like the worst day ever, but first of all, Daddy is fine, and second, I just know that Smoky will be back. Cats love to sneak away sometimes. I once had a cat that disappeared for two whole weeks and then came home." She sat down on the edge of my bed. "I just got up from a nap. I was pooped." She lay back. Her feet, covered in striped slouchy socks, dangled above the floor. Mom looked like a big mountain with her stomach up in the air like that. "I pulled a post-baby chicken pie out of the freezer for dinner," she said. "It's heating up for us now."

I heard a soft sound from the closet. A teeny tiny *mmmm*.

I sucked in my breath.

"Yes, *yum!*" Mom struggled a bit before she was able to push herself upright.

"What's a post-baby chicken pie?" I asked.

"I've been stockpiling dinners to freeze and made a bunch of homemade chicken pies. After the baby is born, life will be easier if I can just pull supper out of the freezer."

I nodded. "True."

"I'm excited to try one tonight. It's a super healthy chicken pie recipe. Good thing, because the doctor told your dad today to knock it off with his bad eating habits. Now it isn't just me nagging."

Mom stood up. She grabbed a sweater that was slung over the back of my chair and carried it to the closet.

"I'll hang that up," I said. "You should go rest."

"I feel fine. I just woke up. Besides, I'm nesting." She winked at me.

I knew all about nesting. Pregnant ladies liked to start cooking and cleaning before their babies came. It was like some weird reaction for readying themselves. I'd seen her do it before.

Mom reached for the knob on the closet door.

"Wait!" I yelled.

Her head whipped around. "What?!" Her hand flew up to her chest. "Gosh, Lizzy! You scared me!"

"I'm sorry. It's just that . . . you shouldn't be picking up after me."

"Were you going to hang it up yourself?" Mom raised her eyebrows and gave me a doubting look. "I appreciate you doting on me, but I'm fine."

I grabbed the sweater out of her hands. "You should be

relaxing. Especially after working."

"I didn't work much today, remember?"

"Well, I can hang up my own stuff." I stood there gripping the sweater so tightly my fingers looked pale.

"Fine," she said. Then she pulled the closet door wide open and swung her arm toward the inside like people do when they say *after you*.

I gasped. Fudge peeked in. And Charlotte made a little yelping noise.

"What is it?" Mom asked, still looking my way and not in the closet.

"Nothing," I said hurrying awkwardly in front of her so I was half blocking her view. I could see Charlotte was pushed back as far as she could go behind my bathrobe, which, thankfully, was so long it hung to the floor. But I saw part of one foot sticking out. And the blankets and pillows that were Charlotte's so-called bed. "I . . . I . . . just remembered homework stuff, that's all."

Mom grabbed a hanger. "Here you go." She handed it to me. "Why don't you eat first, then do homework? You'll think better on a full stomach."

I was dying to close the door, but Mom's giant tummy was in the way. Which was also hopefully blocking her view of the floor. Charlotte obviously had no clue her foot was showing, because she didn't try to move it out of sight. The longer we stood there with the door open, the bigger Charlotte's toes seemed to grow.

"Okay," I said. "Do you think dinner's ready now?"

"About twenty minutes."

Move out of the way! I wanted to scream at the toes and my mother.

Then Mom looked straight into my closet. I saw her eyes widen.

My throat closed.

"You should go through your clothes. Surely you've outgrown some of these things." She pulled at some of my tops and sweaters hanging just inches from my robe. "Why don't we donate the stuff that doesn't fit you to someone who could wear it?"

There wasn't even a sip of air left in my lungs. I tried to take a deep breath.

"Oh my goodness!" Mom squealed. Just when I thought I might pass out, she turned to face me. "What's the matter with me? Pregnancy brain! I came in here to tell you something important!"

"What?" I asked.

"Sergeant Blumstein is stopping by tonight."

"What for?"

"I suppose he wants to ask us if we noticed anything unusual the day of the fire."

"I didn't see anything," I said quickly. "Are you sure it's about the fire?"

"What else could it be about?" She smiled. "It's possible that one of us might have seen something that seemed like no biggie to us, but might be meaningful to the police and fire department."

"'Kay," was all I managed to say because a train wreck was piling up inside me.

Mom seemed to notice how nervous I was. "You don't need to worry about Sergeant Blumstein. It's not like you have anything to hide."

She left and shut the door.

And from the closet, in the tiniest voice, I heard the words, "Except for me."

CHAPTER 17

"WHAT WERE YOU DOING IN THE TRIPLE DECKER Saturday morning?" Sergeant Blumstein leaned over the kitchen table in front of me. My parents stood, one on each side of him—two crazy-eyed bookends.

"Lizzy! Were you inside that house?" My mother reached across Blumstein and grabbed at my father's arm in a panic.

"Inside the house? When?" Dad asked.

"Let me make this clear up front," Blumstein said. "I'm not accusing Lizzy of having anything to do with the fire, but she was seen coming out a window of that house on Saturday morning just after nine thirty."

"Lizzy!" my mother practically shouted. "Why?" Her face turned as white as the kitchen cabinets.

"Which Saturday?" I said. Which was about the dumbest

answer ever. I had sort of just admitted that I had snuck into the house another time, even though I hadn't. And was Blumstein just pretending that he didn't think I had started the fire? Was he trying to trick me? Was this about Charlotte? Had someone seen her going into the apartment, too? I tried to stop my brain from thinking the worst, but apparently my mind had a mind of its own. I pressed my fingers against my temples.

"Lizzy, did you hear the sergeant?" Mom asked. "He said, this past Saturday. The day of the fire." My mother looked like she was about to cry.

"Mom, I didn't do anything wrong. I swear."

"Again," Blumstein said, "I'm not accusing you of setting the fire, though slipping into a building you are clearly supposed to stay out of isn't going to earn you a gold star; ya know what I mean?"

My head nodded so fast it looked like the kitchen was jiggling.

"So the fire was set by someone?" my father interrupted.

"I didn't say that, either, Henry. I said someone saw your daughter coming out of the front window. And I need to be thorough in this investigation before we can definitively say what caused the fire."

My parents and Blumstein stared from across the table, waiting for me to say something. It felt like Team Everybody against Team Lizzy. And how unfair was it that I was the only one seated, since I'd be the one most likely to have to make a run for it?

"Someone saw me? Who?"

Blumstein crossed his arms in front of his chest. When he shifted, the handcuffs hanging from his belt clinked against his clip-on walkie-talkie. In spite of the tsunami-sized wave of fear rising up inside me, I couldn't help noticing that he carried around a lot of equipment.

"Who saw you is not important," he told me.

"They only saw me?" I asked. How stupid could I be? That was like a three-pointer for the other team.

Blumstein pounced on my mistake. "Why? Was there someone else with you?"

I took a deep breath. If this was a scene from a TV show, I would be lawyering up. But then I'd be making myself look guilty. Oh, that's right. I was already doing *that*.

"Lizzy." Sergeant Blumstein said my name like it tasted bad. He raised his eyebrows. *Cut to the chase*, those bushy things seemed to be saying.

"Nope," I lied. "There wasn't anyone with me. But if there was someone with me, then the person who saw me was mistaken because they said I was alone." Yikes! That made about as much sense as a toothless comb. I definitely didn't operate well when I was nervous. And now I knew what a sideways look meant by the one Dad shot at me from across the table.

"Lizzy," Dad said. He swiped at his hair. "Was Joss with you?"

Seriously? Thrown under the bus by my own father.

"Are they sure it was me?" I asked.

Blumstein sighed. "Well, were you there?"

"Lizzy. Tell the truth. This is important," Mom said. "Sergeant Blumstein just wants your help. That's all, right?" she asked him. She rubbed her big belly. This was stressing her out. Stress wasn't good for the baby.

The ice maker kicked on, and I heard the *plink* sound of ice dropping into the plastic bucket inside the freezer. *Plink. Plink. Plink. Plink. Plink. Plink. Plink.* I don't know why, in the middle of all this, I was thinking that ice making and microwaving popcorn were kind of alike. Kernels popped like crazy all at once until the final few spaced-out pops. Ice did that, too, in its own way. Plinking all at once until the ice bin was full, and then the few final cubes dropping. I listened for more plinks.

If three more cubes dropped, that was a sign to tell the truth.

Plink.

If less than three dropped . . .

. . . *Plink* . . .

. . . deny everything.

I waited for the sound of a third plink.

That was it. Just the two.

"It wasn't me," I said.

Then, *plink.*

"Okay, I did go inside. But just to look for Smoky." *Plink. Plink. Plink.* Uh-oh. What did six cubes dropping mean?

"Who's Smoky?" Blumstein asked. He looked excited, like I had uncovered a new clue.

"A cat," Mom, Dad, and I all answered together.

"Interesting name, considering the circumstances," Blumstein said.

"I snuck in through the window because I wanted to feed him and see if he had kittens. Well, I didn't know he was a he at the time; I thought he was a she. But she turned out to be a he, and there were no kittens, because, you know . . ." I felt myself blush.

"Why didn't you just say that right off the bat?" he asked me.

"I was scared I'd get in trouble for going inside the house."

"Was Joss with you?" he asked.

"Yes. We both went inside." If I was reading the sign right, six plinks meant six truths. He had two more questions, according to the ice cubes.

"Did you notice anything unusual when you were inside?"

"Not really. Except that the front room was really sunny, but the rest of the house was pretty dark. That was a little weird."

"Did you see lots of leaves around?"

"Yes. Tons of them."

Blumstein rubbed his chin. I knew that rub from all his trips to the diner. His thinking rub. It usually followed the question *Doughnut or danish?*

"And you are sure you didn't see anything unusual in the house?"

"I'm sure. Positive." Technically that was the truth because the house itself seemed totally and completely usual. Except for the sunny room with the big windows, the rest of the place looked like what an old, rundown apartment should look like. A little creepy. A dirty tub, a worn-out chair, a few broken windows. Now, if he had asked me if I had seen any*one* unusual in the house, well, that was a different story. Because it wasn't very usual at all to find a person living inside a closet of a house no one was supposed to be living in.

"Lizzy, did the two of you play with matches inside that house?"

"NO! I swear!" And that was two answers more than the ice cubes told me I had to answer.

"I thought you didn't think Lizzy had anything to do with the fire," my father said.

"The question needed to be asked, Henry."

"We only fed the cat and then went straight to the Thumbs-Up to eat and work," I said. "Remember? We saw you there."

Blumstein nodded. He stared at me for a few seconds. Did he believe me? Did he know about Charlotte hiding out in the apartment, but wasn't saying?

"They were at the diner all day, the both of them, bussing tables up until the fire started," my father added.

"All right then," Sergeant Blumstein said. "I think we're good." He looked at my mother. "What do you got for danish tomorrow?"

"Apricot," she said. "Dan, the house burned after three in the afternoon, and she was there much, much earlier in the morning."

"Yes. And I believe Lizzy."

"Really?" I said out loud. I had meant to say it only to myself.

"Of course. After I heard Lizzy was spotted inside, I wouldn't be doing my job if I didn't come here and ask some questions . . . cross the *T*s and dot the *I*s, you know?" Sergeant Blumstein smiled at me. "First of all, it doesn't make one bit of sense to me that two young girls would get up early on a Saturday morning to light matches in an old house before they had to get to work. But the stray cat story makes a whole lot of sense."

The color in my mom's cheeks came back.

"As a matter of fact, though, we did find some moldy matches . . . in the fireplace. We thought maybe someone had gone in that empty house and tried to light a fire to keep warm."

I sat up straighter.

"But the inspectors found the matches had never been lit," he continued. "And the fireplace and chimney were virtually unscathed. There hadn't been a fire burned there in years. Besides, the fire started nowhere near the fireplace."

I felt myself relax to the point I thought I might slide off my chair.

"So how do you think it started?" my mother asked. "Arson?"

"Nope. No trace of accelerant," Blumstein said.

That meant Charlotte's mom's client didn't do it.

"I wondered about someone burning leaves outside," my father said. "A couple of good sparks from a pile of dried leaves and *poof*!"

Blumstein shook his head no. "It did not start outside. But leaves were definitely a factor. The fire started from the inside on the floor, almost as you enter that front room. There are significant burn marks. We can see how the fire spread from there. The place was full of dried leaves, and that played a part in the building catching so quickly."

"I wonder what sparked it," my mother said.

"There was a large mirror over the fireplace, and glass knobs on the doors. Based on where we know the fire first started, the fire chief is certain that sunlight and glass refracting incinerated those leaves."

I knew what he was talking about. *Refraction.* I was a Girl Scout for about a week, because that's all it took for me to know I wasn't scout material. But in that short time, I once used the sun and a magnifying glass to start a fire and fry an egg on a tin can.

Mom seemed so relieved that she was putting together a plate of cookies like it was time to celebrate.

"I guess burn marks tell a story," my dad said.

"Indeed they do," said Blumstein. "It's certainly not the first time refraction has started a fire. And the evidence proves that being the cause here. Case closed," he said, reaching for a cookie.

Which meant I was off the hook and so was Charlotte. She was free to go home. Right now. Before the baby came. Taking all the good luck she had brought with her away.

CHAPTER
18

I WOKE UP KNOWING TWO THINGS.

First, the name of a new sandwich special inspired by last night's hairy meeting with Sergeant Blumstein: The Hot Seat. Hot pastrami, pepper jack cheese, and spicy mustard on a grilled bun.

And second, that I needed to convince Charlotte to let us contact her parents and let them know that she was okay.

I yawned and threw my covers off. We'd been up late again last night. Charlotte was worried about Blumstein's visit, even though I had told her a million times she had nothing to worry about. I explained that he had only wanted to ask me why I had been in the apartment house. And that was the truth. The thing is, she *would* have believed she had nothing to worry about if I had told her about the refraction part. But I hadn't. Because I needed her to stick around.

I grabbed the Heart the World posters that Charlotte had made. It must have taken her so long to draw all those tiny red hearts. There wasn't a single one I could see that she hadn't colored in perfectly. None of the hearts looked sad or angry like her own heart felt. Charlotte had been so worried last night that I decided to wait until this morning to tell her about my idea to send an e-mail to her parents. I slipped a rubber band around the poster and tucked it into an outside pocket of my bag.

"Hey!" I whispered, leaning over her. But she didn't move. I lowered myself to the floor. "Charlotte! Charlotte! Wake up!" At that same moment, the door to the diner shut hard and the closet floor shimmied a bit. Charlotte's eyes fluttered. Then they opened. She stared straight up at the ceiling for a few seconds. She looked like she was trying to remember where she was.

"What's wrong?" she asked, springing upright. "Why did you wake me up? It's so early." She rubbed her eyes. "Now my boring day will be so much longer."

"Sorry, but this is important."

Charlotte's red bangs stuck up in every direction, like she had been electrocuted. It made me smile.

"What's funny?" she asked.

"Your hair looks cute," I told her.

"That's not why you woke me up, is it? To tell me my hair looks cute?" She patted it down as best as she could. "What time is it?"

"My bus is coming soon, so listen," I said. "I couldn't sleep last night. I couldn't stop thinking about Smoky."

"He's just scared. He'll come back. It's not like you don't know where he is."

"That's my point exactly. The same can't be said about you. You're gone. Like the cat. Except your parents have no idea where you are. Think about it—if we both feel so upset about Smoky, and we *know* where he is, how do you think your parents feel?"

Charlotte blinked. Twice. Then finally said, "My father ditched us first." Her mouth clamped shut into a straight line. She didn't need to say any more. I knew what she was thinking. That was the whole point of her running away in the first place. To hurt them like they had hurt her. She wanted them to be worried.

"Yeah, but your mom and brother and sister didn't run out on you. Now you and your dad have both ditched them."

Charlotte didn't seem to know what to say to that. I continued, "Your parents must be crazy out of their minds worrying. Why don't you give me your mom's e-mail address? I'll do it. I can sneak and use one of the computers at school. It might be traceable to my school, but they can't trace it to *me*."

Charlotte nodded. "What will you say?"

"I'll tell your family that you're okay. That nothing bad has happened to you. That's all. That's what they want to know. Trust me. I know what it feels like to have something gone that you love."

She probably thought I meant my cat. What else would she think?

I thought back to my mother after the car accident. After we lost the baby. When Bibi helped with the laundry or drove me places when Mom wouldn't get out of bed. And all those silent dinners at the table when she finally did. The dumb jokes I used to tell to try to make her laugh. Sometimes I'd babble on about nothing just to suck up the silence.

"Are you crying about Smoky?" Charlotte asked me.

I hadn't realized my face was streaked with tears. I quickly wiped them away. She looked at me like she suddenly realized that maybe I was hiding more than just a girl inside my closet.

"Give me your mom's contact info," I said, sniffing. I grabbed a pen off my desk and a scrap of paper and handed them to her.

"Only if you promise me something," she said.

"What?"

"Promise first."

"I promise. What is it?"

"You can send the e-mail to my mom. But *write* the e-mail to Molly and Ethan. Not to my parents. And tell the twins I miss them. A lot."

• • •

Mrs. Potter took her lunch break in the teacher's lounge every day at 11:45 a.m., and everyone who walked by the lounge knew it. It seemed she only liked food that smelled like fish or garlic. That meant two things: one, you were super unlucky if your computer class fell after her lunch; and two, the computer room was empty at 11:48 when I slipped inside and closed the door behind me.

I had to beg and fake cry to convince Ms. Santorelli to let me check on Smoky one more time.

"Don't take advantage of my good nature," she had warned me. "You've checked twice already. Make it quick." But there was nothing quick about our dinosaur computers that took forever just to power on.

East Thumb isn't a fancy town with fancy schools, and if anyone didn't know it, all they had to do was pay a visit to our computer lab. The computers are fat and square and slower than sleepy turtles. That didn't bother me on a regular day, but it was making me a nervous wreck right now. I waited for the logon screen to appear.

The door opened, and I jumped out of my seat.

"Bathroom break!" Joss said, closing the door quickly behind her.

"You scared me," I said, sitting back down.

"No Smoky sighting still?" she asked, glancing at the hole.

"No."

"What did you say in the e-mail?"

"Nothing yet," I said. "This thing is so slow."

Joss leaned in over my shoulder toward the screen. We both waited silently, watching the small white circle spinning to let us know the page was loading. Finally everything turned blue and icons popped up everywhere. I clicked on the one that said MAIL.

"I'm keeping the e-mail super short, like, *Dear Molly and Ethan, Charlotte misses you a lot.* Do you think that's enough?"

"I know you promised her you wouldn't say anything to her parents, but maybe you could tell the twins to tell their parents not to worry, too."

"Her parents are the ones who will get the e-mail. They'll know she's okay," I said.

"I don't know," Joss said. "An e-mail to just her brother and sister with only nine words sounds kind of cold. And weird since it sounds like someone else is writing it, not Charlotte. Her parents might think you're like, a bad guy, or something. You should make it sound like she's writing it."

"Really?" I asked.

"Yes. Otherwise they will think she was kidnapped and not that she ran away."

"No, they won't. She left a note," I said.

"She could have been kidnapped after she ran away."

I typed in Charlotte's mother's e-mail address. "Okay. How about this instead? *I am fine and not too hungry. I miss Molly and Ethan.* Should I add that she's safe and warm?"

Joss made her thinking face. "How about, *I am inside a house*?"

"No, I don't want to say that. What if they start searching all the houses in East Thumb?"

"You think they'd do that?"

"They might. I mean, they probably would," I said.

"I don't know. They'd have to search every single house of every single student and teacher. And some of the teachers don't even live in East Thumb."

"I guess." I shrugged. I didn't know what the police protocol was for a runaway. But her parents were lawyers. They could probably get the police to search if they asked them to.

"Okay. This is what I have," I said. *"Dear Molly and Ethan, I am fine. I am warm, fed, and safe. I miss you both a lot.* That's nineteen words. Better?"

"Much," Joss said.

I was just about to hit SEND, but I stopped myself. "Whoa!" I said. A prickly feeling shot through both my hands as my nerves exploded. I shut the computer down fast.

"What are you doing?" Joss asked.

"The time is on the e-mail!" I looked up at the clock. "We're the only ones in here at 12:01. The e-mail would be traced to me, for sure."

Joss slapped her hand over her mouth. "So how are you going to send a message?" she asked me through her fingers.

"We have to send it from a computer that can't be traced to us."

The door swung open, and Ms. Santorelli stuck her head in. "Girls!" she said in a voice that tried to be angry. Even with her forehead all crunched up, she wasn't very good at being mad. "I don't like being taken advantage of."

"Sorry," I said.

"I was okay with you coming to check on your cat, but what are you doing fooling around on the computer?"

"I'm not. I'm just sitting here. While I wait." If a white lie was considered harmless and a bold-faced lie was the opposite of harmless, I had just gray lied. A gray lie was in between. Bottom line, I hadn't really accomplished anything on the computer, and anyway, right now I truly was just sitting in front of it.

"And you." She pointed at Joss. "You're not supposed to be in here at all."

"I'm sorry. I just wanted to help Lizzy."

"Let's go. Clearly the cat is not ready to come out. You're better off coming back later in the evening when the school is empty. Mrs. Potter has a class in eight minutes."

I had enough experience with cats to know that was true. At least, that was usually the case. A lot of cats got spooked when there was noise or sensed a lot of commotion going on. Not Fudge so much. But definitely Reuben, and apparently Smoky.

But so far, even when the school was practically empty and we were super quiet, it hadn't mattered.

I looked over my shoulder to check one more time before I closed the door. I saw a black hole and nothing else.

CHAPTER
19

IT WAS A QUICK TRIP TO THE PORTLAND PUBLIC Library. It took just ten minutes to send the e-mail to Molly and Ethan, even though it was technically sent to Charlotte's mother. It would serve its purpose of letting her whole family know she was safe.

We sped down 95 on the 4:05 bus out of Portland, taking us back to East Thumb.

"Have you noticed that no one has come up with a Heart the World project since our cat sweater presentation bombed? Instead of inspiring the rest of the class like Ms. Santorelli had hoped we would, we probably did the opposite. I bet the Heart the World thing tanks and that board in the classroom stays empty. Don't you think?" Joss was asking.

"It's only been two days," I said.

"Yeah . . . but jeez . . . it seems like the only one we inspired was Smoky . . . to hide out in fear for the rest of his life. Good thing he has nine of them. Well, seven now, if you count him surviving the streets and escaping the fire."

I nodded. I watched the pine trees whip by. The sky was gray. *Gloomy.* A sign of what I was feeling.

"How come you're so quiet?" Joss asked me.

"Just thinking about stuff," I said.

"You don't need to worry anymore about Charlotte's parents. When they get the e-mail that she's safe, they'll feel so much better. And nobody we know saw us at the Portland library."

Sending the e-mail from East Thumb was not an option. Our public library has only one large room, one computer, and one librarian, Mr. Keith, who knows everyone in town.

I was glad we had let Charlotte's parents know that she was okay. It was the least I could do since I hadn't told Charlotte everything I had learned about how the apartment house burned down. Maybe she wouldn't want to go home yet, anyway, even if she did know she had nothing to do with the fire. She changed her mind a lot. . . . One minute she was mad . . . the next she was sad and homesick. Still, it was for her to decide when to leave, not me.

"So what are you worried about?" Joss was asking. "I can tell it's something."

"Am I a terrible person?" I asked her.

"Why are you even asking me that?"

I had told Joss everything about the meeting with Blumstein, except the part about the cause of the fire.

"Promise me you won't tell Charlotte," I said.

"Tell Charlotte what?"

Before she even promised me she'd keep it a secret, I blurted it out. Then I added, "I don't want her to leave yet."

"Wow," Joss said. "Refraction . . . it was the sun's fault?"

I nodded. "So. Now do you think I'm a terrible person?"

She didn't say anything for a few seconds, and I squirmed a bit in my seat.

"Actually, you're the opposite of terrible," she finally said. "If it wasn't for you, Charlotte would be out on the streets! Do you ever think about what could have happened to her if that were the case?"

"Maybe she would have already gone back home," I said.

"You'll never know that for sure. At least she's been safe. But you *do* know for sure . . . Charlotte can't stay forever. I mean, I know you know that she can't stay for infinity, duh, but . . . the baby isn't coming for another month and a half. That's a really long time for her to be away from her family. Never mind living in a closet. Hello?"

"I know." I sighed. My breath made a foggy stain on the window.

Joss reached over me and traced a tic-tac-toe board on the cold glass. "FYI," she said, "a terrible person wouldn't worry if they were a terrible person. But a not-at all-terrible person would." She made an *X* in the center square. "Your turn."

I drew an *O* in one of the spaces. We went back and forth, but there was no winner. That felt like a bad sign.

• • •

It was four fifteen when we pulled into the bus station. We ran the two blocks to The Community Lodge for Cats & Dogs. Mom was picking us up at the shelter at 5:30 p.m. and bringing cat food to drop off at school for Smoky on our way home.

The shelter dogs barked like mad when we jogged past them.

"Hey, girls," Phil shouted to us from inside a kennel. He was refilling water bowls. His hair was still blue.

We waved. "Hi, Phil," I said.

A husky jogged to the fence to get a closer look at us. "Hi, cutie." I blew a kiss at his white furry face. I wished I could take the husky and every one of the dogs home with me. But Mom already said with Smoky, we were at capacity.

Inside, a giant basket of laundry was waiting for us. Joss picked it up and I followed her to the basement where the washing machine was. I measured detergent while Joss dropped the dirty blankets and sheets into the drum.

"What's Franny's secret?" my mom liked to tease. "You do all that laundry at the shelter and I can't even get you to put your dirty clothes in a hamper!"

Back upstairs, Franny was behind the counter filling out the whiteboard. She was writing in the names of the kittens that would be going to the vet over the next couple of days.

"Hello there," she said to us. "Can you grab a couple of carriers, please?" She held up two fingers. All of her fingers were stacked up to the knuckles with rings, even her thumbs. She let us count them once. Twenty-three!

"Those four baby girls are heading out in the morning to be chipped and spayed," Franny told us.

She handed us markers and a roll of masking tape. "Annabelle and Mimi on one. Emmy and Boo-Boo on the other," Franny said, as we labeled the crates.

"I like their names," Joss said.

"They certainly are sweet," Franny said.

Joss unzipped her backpack and pulled out a Cozy Cat sweater. "Speaking of sweet . . . hel-lo!" She swung the sweater over her head.

"Oh my gracious, let me see that!" Franny held the sweater up against Zuma before handing it back to Joss. "Adorable! Zuma needs extra-large."

"It's one size fits all," Joss said. "They're totally stretchy."

Next to the front door, I hung up the poster Charlotte had made. Joss pinned the sweater beside it. "We'll leave this sample so anyone who comes into the shelter will see it," she said.

"Perfect," Franny said.

Joss and I fist-bumped. "We've sold three sweaters already," I told her. "And those are just the ones we got paid for and have delivered. But we have lots more orders."

"I'll be there on Saturday around ten-ish. Phil can hold down the fort here for an hour or so."

"Do you have the Marco pictures?" I asked Joss. "Let's put one up next to the poster."

For publicity purposes we had planned to take pictures of Smoky wearing a Cozy Cat sweater that day at school, but of course it hadn't happened. So Joss had taken a few pictures of her cat Marco wearing one.

Marco looked super peeved to be wearing the sweater, with his ears flattened back. In one of the pictures it looked like he was trying to bite Elle's arm. He wasn't a good candidate for the job.

"I told you we should have used Fudge," I said.

"This one isn't too bad." Joss pointed to a picture of Marco slung over Elle's shoulder facing away from the camera. Even though his ears were still flat you couldn't see his face and how annoyed he really was.

Joss put the photo up next to the sweater. I wrote in the prices where I could find space on the poster without ruining Charlotte's art. When we finished, we still had time before my mom came to visit with the cats and see the new kittens.

I peered through the glass window of the cat room. "Awww, look at them," I said, pointing to one racing after a small ball. "Come on," I said to Joss.

We closed the door behind us just as a bunch of cats ran over to greet us. Some meowed.

"Hi, everyone," I called out. "Did you miss us?" I petted all the ones that had gathered around my legs.

The first thing Joss and I liked to do was to read all the names on the outside of the cages to see who had gone home and who was still there. It always made me feel good to see names I didn't recognize, because that meant others had found a forever home.

There was one large window in the room and underneath it a carpet-covered window seat where the cats liked to bask in the sun during the day. The floor was cement and covered with small area rugs, toys, scratching posts, bright-colored bowls of water, and litter boxes. A lot of the cats liked the "trees," which were tall carpet-covered structures for climbing and lounging.

I picked up one of the orange kittens and Joss held one of the black ones and we sat down on a rug.

"She has a little beard." Joss pressed the kitten gently to her face.

I kissed the kitten I was holding on the top of its head and stroked its tiny triangle of an ear. Joss and I took turns with all four of them so they each got an equal amount of love and kisses. Then we turned our attention to the rest of the cats, playing with them, tickling bellies, and scratching backs. Only Trudy couldn't come out of her cage, which made me feel bad until I saw that she was sound asleep.

We refilled the water bowls and scooped a couple of the boxes that needed cleaning before we said good-bye to the cats and went back out front to wash our hands.

While we waited for my mom, I told Franny about Smoky.

"Stop putting food out," she said.

"He'll starve!" I said.

"Oh, no he won't. He's having some fun with you. He's smarter than you think. The inside of that wall probably feels like a palace to him. He waits for the coast to be clear and when it is, he gobbles up his dinner and goes back inside that cozy hole."

"It's mean to take away his food," Joss said.

"Nope," Franny said, "it's not. Ever hear of the cat and the fiddle?"

"Yeah," I said.

"Well, he's the cat, and Lizzy's the fiddle." Franny winked at me. "He's playing you like one. Trust me. He'll come out looking for food. And when he doesn't find it, he'll come looking for some-one to get it for him."

I sure hoped she was right.

CHAPTER
20

By Thursday, Smoky still hadn't come out, but more horrible stuff was waiting for me at school.

"I want my money back," Cooper said. He pushed up his sleeve. His arm had a long, bloody scratch on it.

"Whoa. What happened?" I asked.

"Your stupid cat sweater. That's what happened. I tried to put it on my cat and he tried to kill me. Look at these." Cooper yanked the top of his shirt down and showed me three ugly scratches.

"Wow," was all I could think of to say. I thought about Sid and Phil both telling me that sweater-wearing cats might be risky.

"Well, we don't do refunds," Joss said. "It's for charity."

"I don't care. I want my money back."

"It's not our fault your cat is nuts," Joss said.

"My cat is not nuts. Your idea is dumb."

"Hold on, you guys," I said. "It's fine. We'll give you back your money."

"Lizzy!" Joss said.

I pulled her to the side and whispered, "We don't want him to be mad, okay? He'll tell the whole school not to buy our cat sweaters. Let's just give him back his ten dollars."

"Fine. But give us back the sweater and the shelter decal or you're not getting your money," she told Cooper. She marched off in a huff.

Cooper pulled the sweater out of his backpack. "I don't want it, anyway," he said, handing it over to me.

"I don't have any money with me today, but I'll bring your ten dollars tomorrow."

"Don't forget," he told me.

"I won't. And you can keep the decal. Sorry it didn't work out." I felt bad that he was all scratched up. And worse that the cat didn't like wearing our sweater.

As if reading my mind, Cooper said, "Your own cat doesn't want to wear one. He's scared if he comes out of the wall that you'll make him."

The bell sounded, and Zoe sprinted into the room, pulling some kind of metal contraption on wheels behind her. She dropped a cat sweater on my desk on the way to her seat.

"Here," she said, "You can keep the money as a donation, but my cousin doesn't want the sweater. Rocco bit her when she tried to put it on him."

"Seriously?" I heard Joss say.

Zoe parked the contraption by her seat and went to the back of the room to put up a poster on the Heart the World board.

"What do we have here?" Ms. Santorelli smiled. Most of us swiveled around in our seats to get a look at the poster Zoe was tacking up.

"Port-a-cycle," Zoe told us as she pinned it into the cork.

"Like a port-a-potty?" Cooper asked.

"Nope. Well, maybe a little bit. It is portable. But it's not a potty." A tall trash can made of wire was strapped to a dolly with a bunch of bungee cords. Zoe pulled it to the front of the class. "My idea for Heart the World is to help some of the older people around East Thumb get their recyclables out to the curb for pickup day. I load their bottles and newspapers in here." She waved her hand over the opening of the trash bin like a game-show host showing off a new car. "Then I wheel all the recyclables out to the curb for them and toss everything in their bin."

"Just out of curiosity, why wouldn't you just lug their own bins to the curb in the first place?" Cooper asked.

Zoe looked stunned. "I like my idea better," she said. "My bin has wheels." She pulled the port-a-cycle back to her seat and sat down.

"It's fantastic, Zoe. Remember," Ms. Santorelli told the class, "the purpose of Heart the World is to do something kind for somebody. Pay it forward! And our board is still pretty empty. Let's see if we can fill it up. There are lots of ways to love the world, people!"

But the concept of loving the world wasn't working out so well for Joss and me. We were trying to pay it forward, but everything seemed to be moving backward for us. By lunch, everyone but Ms. Santorelli had canceled their sweater orders. And most of the customers that actually had a sweater for their cat were showing off their bite marks and bloody scratches.

"This stinks!" Joss said.

"No kidding. I mean, our fund-raiser at the diner is Saturday. No one will show up. We have to cancel."

"Or we could just try to sell them, anyway," Joss said.

"No, we can't do that," I told her. "That would be shady, knowing what we know about all the scratches. Plus, this is a small town. Word spreads fast."

"There goes all the money we were going to raise." Joss dropped her face down on the small pile of sweaters. "What a waste."

"Wait. Get up," I said. "Give me one of those sweaters."

"Here. Take them all."

"You know how cats love to sit on things . . . a piece of paper, a book? Fudge sits on my computer keys all the time. What if instead of sweaters, we knit blankets for them to lie on?"

Joss smiled. "I knew I loved you for a reason."

"Just one reason?" I fake frowned.

"We don't even have to change the Cozy Cat name. Blankets are cozy."

"Cozier than sweaters!" I said.

"Plus, the blankets will be even faster to knit than the sweaters . . . no leg or head holes!"

There was a loud *clank* and a *splat*. I looked over my shoulder and saw that Zoe had dropped her lunch tray. A pile of mac and cheese had just missed her foot and a puddle of red fruit juice was spreading out across the floor. I watched it flow into a wide heart-like shape.

"Look!" I whispered to Joss. "Do you see that?" I pointed to the red juice.

"Yeah. I'm glad I'm not the one who has to clean up that mess."

"Not that," I said. "The way the juice is flowing. Do you see? It's making a giant red heart on the floor."

Joss looked again. "That might be a stretch. I mean, if it is a heart, it's kind of lopsided on one side."

"It's very heart-like," I said. "Plus, it's red."

"Well, the juice was red. I mean, it's not like it magically turned red when it spilled!"

"It's just so weird . . . the whole Heart the World thing . . . and now there's a big heart on the floor. I think it's a sign."

"It's a defective-looking heart, if you ask me. So if it's a sign, it's probably not a very good one."

True that it wasn't a perfectly shaped heart. But it was pretty close. "Real-life hearts aren't perfectly shaped, anyway," I said.

Joss shrugged her shoulders and wiped jelly off her mouth. "One never knows, I guess," she said.

Cooper came over with a bunch of napkins and helped Zoe clean up the mess. I watched the heart disappear.

Back in the classroom, I made a few edits to the poster we had hung up on the Heart the World board and wrote in the word *blanket* over the crossed-out word *sweater*.

Joss made an announcement to the class and asked everyone to spread the news about the cat blankets so that people would show up to our event Saturday.

"Okay, well, I guess you can keep my ten dollars if I get a blanket now," Cooper told us.

"Yay!" I said.

The afternoon dragged on because I wanted to get home and start knitting the blankets and let Charlotte know the new plan. Plus, we had sweater posters at the shelter that we needed to change. I had to call Franny and tell her. I wiggled in my seat a bit and tried to focus on the discussion about Mesopotamia. When I looked up, Ms. Santorelli stopped speaking. She looked at me with her eyebrows raised and her eyes pulled wide open. She pointed at me. I sat up straighter. Right away I thought, *busted*. She could tell I wasn't paying one bit of attention.

"Everyone stay in your seats and keep quiet," she said in a hushed voice. We all turned to watch when she sprinted on tiptoes to shut the classroom door. Then she grabbed Smoky's carrier, which had been sitting in a corner of the classroom since Monday.

That's when I looked down at my feet.

Smoky! I had almost shouted but I stopped myself. I made a happy little squeak instead. He was right under my desk! My cat was back! He curled around my leg. Someone else must have spotted him, too, because they announced: "The cat is back!"

The rest of the class burst into a unified cheer. Smoky froze, his front paws splayed out a bit, his tail puffed up, and his ears pointed back.

Ms. Santorelli shushed everyone. "Do not spook him." The room got quiet.

"He's afraid," I said softly. Ms. Santorelli placed the carrier by my desk. Smoky came closer and sniffed at it. That's when I reached down and pulled him up onto my lap. I pressed him against my chest. "It's okay, Smoky. I'm sorry you're scared. You've been lost and found two times in less than a week, silly boy." I rested my cheek on the top of his head. The whole class watched in silence when I slowly slid out of my chair and kneeled by the carrier. I had barely opened the little door when Smoky scurried in quickly, as if he couldn't wait to get home. He curled up in a ball and stared out at me with his celery-green eyes.

"News flash," Cooper said. "Don't try to put one of your dumb sweaters on him."

"They're blankets now," I reminded him as I turned the little lock. I pulled on the door to double-check that it was secure.

"Franny was right! Taking his food away worked!" Joss was saying.

"He's hungry," I said.

Ms. Santorelli fed him some cheese from her lunch. I texted my mom to tell her the good news, and to ask her to pick Smoky and me up after school.

All of a sudden my day wasn't so horrible. Saturday's fund-raising event was back on. Smoky was coming home. And that random weird-shaped heart. It meant something. Something big, I was sure.

CHAPTER
21

"STOP!" I SCREAMED.

Mom slammed on the brakes in front of the diner, and Smoky's cage almost slid off my lap. "Oh my goodness, Lizzy, what is it?"

"What is that?" I asked, pointing at the front window of the Thumbs-Up. But I could see what it was. More importantly, who it was.

"What?" my mother repeated.

"Who put that poster there?" I opened the car door, not taking my eyes off the photo of Charlotte staring out from the diner window. Her pale face looked like a small moon shining through the glass.

"Lizzy! What are you doing?"

"I just want to see."

"Hold on. Let me park the car," Mom told me. I closed the door, and she pulled into the alley. We stepped out onto the sidewalk.

"When did this get put up?" I asked. I assumed it must have been today when I was at school, because there was no way I would have missed it waiting for the bus.

"Oh, it's so sad. This young girl ran away."

"They think she's here?" I was trying to keep my voice steady.

"She's from Lewiston. But she took a bus to East Thumb, so they are looking for her here, yes. Her parents, of course, are just devastated. They came to East Thumb to put up posters and hand out flyers."

"Her parents? Together?"

"Yes. They were in the diner briefly. They came in to ask if it was okay to post the sign. My heart just breaks for them."

"Maybe she came here by bus, but then she left for someplace else."

"Well, maybe. I guess they don't know for sure," Mom said. "But East Thumb is a starting point. The bus station has security cameras, and the Lewiston police tracked when the ticket was purchased, which was last Friday, almost a week ago. Thankfully, they could get that information," my mother said.

Cameras?

"I had seen it reported on the news. I sure hope she's safe."

"I'm sure she's safe," I said.

Mom looked at me and tipped her head to the side. "You're a positive thinker like me, Lizzy."

Well, I'm pretty positive about that.

"She's so lovely. That red hair would be hard not to notice." Mom stared at the poster.

There was that glassy look in her eyes again. My heart clenched like a fist. It's weird for a gaze to feel familiar. But it was. I knew it, because I had seen it on my mom before. There was sadness behind it. That wrecking ball–sadness when something is lost. Like a runaway you can't find. Or a baby that you had been waiting for.

• • •

"Guess who is back?" I announced quietly, as I entered my bedroom.

Charlotte peeked out from the closet. "Smoky!" I put him down, and he scampered over to her. Charlotte picked him up. "He's still so skinny," she said.

"Of course he is. He had only been found a couple days before he was a lost cat again. Not much to eat inside a wall," I said.

"Tell me about it," Charlotte said.

What was that like, being able to relate to a lost cat? Their worlds were strangely similar.

"This is for you." I handed her half of a saved sandwich.

"Thank you."

I had started asking her what she wanted for lunch. "As long as it has yellow mustard and pickles on it, I'm good," she had told me.

While she ate, I noticed she was wearing my clothes. She noticed me noticing.

"I hope you don't mind. I took a shower today," she explained. "I couldn't stand the smell of myself for one day longer."

"That's fine," I said. I was actually relieved. I had noticed her BO a couple of days ago. Joss said it's a favor to tell someone when they stink so they can fix it. But I didn't want to be rude. Still, pregnant people have a strong sense of smell. I didn't want my mom to get a whiff of her and then start sniffing and poking around my closet.

"It was the fastest shower ever. Both your parents were at work."

I nodded. "Your parents have been here looking for you."

Her mouth opened. I saw bits of chewed-up sandwich. "Here? In your house?"

"No. Here in East Thumb. And downstairs, too. There's a giant poster with your face on it in the window of the diner." I explained about the cameras at the bus station.

"I guess I'm glad they're looking for me. Together."

"Of course they would look for you," I said.

Charlotte's eyes lit up like shiny stones. "Did they look like they might still like each other?" she asked.

"I didn't see them. My mom did, though, when they put up the poster."

Charlotte sighed. "I hope my dad changed his mind about leaving us. Maybe my plan worked. I guess I'll find out when I go home," she said.

A tight feeling pulled at the back of my throat.

"If it wasn't for that fire . . . ," she said. "What if they never figure out what started it? I guess if that happens, they won't ever blame me. Except . . . if the bus station cameras prove that I came to East Thumb . . . and when the police find out who owns the apartment house . . . I'd be a suspect. A runaway, a bus ticket to an empty house, a fire . . ." Charlotte covered her mouth with her hand.

"That won't happen," I said.

"How do you know?" she asked.

"I just do. They don't know you were in the house, anyway. I mean, it's possible they have cameras at the Portland Public Library, too."

"So?"

"That's where Joss and I sent your parents the e-mail from. They could trace it, which they probably would, and connect the dots. Joss and I first sneaking into the apartment that was connected to your mother's client, and then being at the library at the same time that e-mail was sent? We'd be suspected of something, too." I hoped not, actually. But I didn't want Charlotte to worry that she was the only one who could get in trouble. "We are all in this together," I told her.

"You can't get in trouble for helping someone," Charlotte said. We looked at each other as if we wished like crazy that was true. Sneaking into a house to feed a cat was one thing. Hiding a human everyone was looking for was something else. "Don't worry," Charlotte continued. "I won't let you get in trouble. I won't tell a soul I was ever here."

"Where will you say you were all this time?" I asked.

"I don't know. I don't even know when I'll be going back at this point. But even if they ever find out I was here, I'll say everything was my idea. Or that you didn't know I was hiding in here."

"I don't think anyone would fall for that," I said.

"My parents are lawyers. They would help you for helping me."

I was thinking they'd want to do just the opposite. Maybe they'd want to put me in jail more than the police. My "helping" was keeping her away from them.

Still, I chose to keep the truth about the fire tucked into a tiny space inside my heart so I couldn't touch it. I needed to keep it there to protect my own family. Otherwise, Charlotte would leave, and who knows what would happen if she took her good luck with her.

"What if I can't ever go home?" Charlotte was asking.

The juice heart that Zoe had spilled popped into my head. What had the shape of it tried to tell me? A sign of a misshapen heart ... a heart that wasn't perfect? *A defective heart* ... Joss had called it ... was that a heart that hid the truth? Like mine?

"I can't stay in this closet forever," Charlotte continued.

"No, you can't. It won't be forever." Then I had an idea. I smiled. "Do you want to take a field trip tonight?"

• • •

My alarm beeped at midnight.

"Are you awake?" I whispered out to Charlotte. No answer.

I opened the closet door. Smoky was snuggled up against her, and they were both sound asleep. Maybe I should just forget about my plan. It seemed risky. But then Charlotte had been excited about it when I told her. And she deserved to have a little fun.

"Hey. Wake up," I shook her gently. Charlotte's eyes opened.

"I'm awake," she said. "Are we going?"

We put sweatshirts and sweatpants over our pajamas, and then jackets and hats and scarves. I wore my fuzzy slippers, and Charlotte wore her sneakers.

"Let's go," I whispered, leading her down the hallway. I grabbed the keys off the hook, and in less than a minute I was unlocking the back door to the diner.

"What are we doing here?" Charlotte asked me as I led her to the kitchen.

"How about a midnight snack?" I asked. I used my phone's flashlight to make our way to the freezer. "We have chocolate, cookie dough, vanilla . . . but we're not sneaking around for just vanilla. You have to have something more exciting than that," I said. "There's Moose Tracks and Oreo, too."

"Wow! I think if I knew all this ice cream was right underneath me I wouldn't be able to sleep, like, ever!"

"You'd get used to it," I said. "But it is pretty awesome."

Charlotte considered each flavor. We had six, mainly because there just wasn't enough room to stock more. Chocolate, vanilla, strawberry, and cookie dough were permanent flavors. But the other two we switched out from time to time. "Can I have a bit of each?" she asked. "But I'll skip the vanilla." She smiled.

"You can have whatever you want," I told her. I grabbed two to-go cups and handed her one. "Go for it," I said, handing her the ice-cream scoop. I held my phone with the light on so she could see. Then she held it for me while I scooped at the cookie dough for myself. By the time we finished we were both shivering. I stuck a plastic spoon into the mound of chocolate that topped Charlotte's mini mountain of flavors.

"I've never hung out in a giant freezer before. It's cool," Charlotte said.

"Cool!" I said. "Get it?" And we both cracked up laughing.

I rinsed off the ice-cream scoop and the spoon we used for the hot fudge, and put them back in the drawer. I wiped the sink dry. "Can't leave any evidence."

"Can I see the rest of the diner?" she asked.

"Of course." I led Charlotte out from the kitchen, past the griddle, and around the counter. "Be careful, don't trip over anything. There are stools on the other side." Even with the moonlight spilling through the windows, and the flashlight from my phone, it was still pretty dark.

"My little brother Ethan would go nuts," Charlotte said when she saw the half car hanging from the ceiling. "He and my dad love old cars. They go to car shows together."

"My dad's not really into cars," I told her. "He just liked it for the diner." I shined the light around the room, and Charlotte took in the old Coke and Pepsi signs, and everything else.

"It's so cute here. When I'm done being a runaway, I'm going to come back and eat here one day." For the first time, that sounded like Charlotte definitely planned to go back home eventually.

"You sort of are eating here right now," I pointed out.

"Kind of. But I'll come back with Molly and Ethan and my mom." She paused. "Too bad my dad won't be with us. He really would have liked the car."

"You can bring him here," I said.

"No. I don't want to." Her voice was angry.

"Hey," I said. "Let's eat our ice cream before it melts."

"Can we sit in one of those amazing booths?"

"No. We better not. We don't want to chance being seen through a window. I have a better idea, anyway."

"What?" she asked.

"It's a surprise." We exited the diner the same way we had sneaked in, through the back. I locked up. Then we hurried in through the other door and up the stairs to my apartment. We stood outside the door, but instead of going in, I grabbed Charlotte's hand and pulled her to the left.

"Where are we going?" she asked.

"You'll see." We stopped in front of another door. I turned the bolt, unlocking it, and pulled. The hinges creaked. In front of us was an iron staircase. "Almost there," I said, licking a glob of fudge off my ice cream. At the top, we reached another door. It was the same width as a regular door but about half as tall.

"Watch your head," I said to Charlotte, ducking.

"What's up here?" She asked, as we stepped outside onto the roof. The wind leaned into us and I held the door as it closed so it wouldn't make a loud bang when it shut.

Charlotte looked around. Her eyes sparkled like they were smiling and happy. It probably felt so good to her to finally spend some time outdoors.

"This is awesome," she said. "Are you allowed up here?"

"We come up here all the time in the summer. My dad calls this place our porch in the sky." The roof was flat where we stood and covered in small stones. The flat area was about as long and wide as a very large swimming pool and was enclosed by an iron railing. The rest of the roof rose up higher behind us, creating a short wall and a perfect spot for the built-in bench next to the door we had just come through.

"Let's eat," I said. We sat with our backs up against the house. Almost immediately I could feel the sting of the cold through my jacket.

"When the weather's warmer, we bring chairs up here, and Mom plants pots of flowers and tomatoes that we serve at the diner. It's like a little garden. Really cute."

"I love it up here," Charlotte said. "We just have a regular boring porch at my house."

"No garden?" I asked.

"No. Just a few flowers by the front steps."

We both shivered. It was cold, especially for eating ice cream, but neither of us cared. We weren't so high up that we could see very far, but the sky was clear, the stars were bright, and there was a fat orange moon between the branches of the trees.

"I'd come up here all the time if I were you. You're lucky."

I was trying to be lucky, I wanted to say. But I didn't.

Instead, neither of us said much. We were too busy eating. I thought about how Charlotte must have seen my life. My two happily married parents. Unlimited free ice cream. A view of the moon from the rooftop. Just the good stuff. That's the way I used to see my life, too, before I knew bad things could happen.

On the night of the car accident, I hadn't paid any attention to the siren I heard earlier that morning. But it had been so loud when the ambulance sped past our apartment, I had to ask Mom to repeat herself.

I said, Mom had repeated in a loud voice, *a special night for just the three of us. You choose the movie.* She had smiled and run her hand down the side of my face and under my chin. She was feeling good. No more morning sickness, finally.

So later that night we made our way to the movie that we never got to see. I remember the scary sound of the crash. Metal crushing and glass smashing. I saw a police car. Its lights flashing. A blue sky at night. My father's blue-lit face. And I heard a siren wailing. The exact same sound I had heard earlier that day. An ambulance. But this one took my mother away. And the baby she was carrying inside her.

CHAPTER 22

"HELLLLLLOOOOO . . . ANYBODY HOME?" CHAR-lotte was asking me. She tapped at my arm, and I pulled my thoughts out of that horrible memory.

"Sorry," I said.

"What's wrong?" she asked me.

"Nothing." I tried to smile, but it wasn't easy, and Charlotte noticed.

"I can tell something is. What is it? Does it have something to do with why you cried the other morning when you asked for my mom's e-mail?"

I didn't answer.

"Well, I guess you don't have to tell me if you don't want to, and it seems like you don't. Not that you don't know every secret about me. Just saying." Charlotte looked away.

She was so right. Not only did I know her secrets, but she trusted me enough to keep them.

"Okay," I said. "I'll tell you."

She waited while I thought of how to start.

"I was in a really bad car accident once," I said.

"I'm sorry," she said. "You're okay now, right?"

"Most of the time," I said. "It still hurts, sometimes."

"What hurts?" she asked me.

I felt the tear run down my cheek.

"Oh," Charlotte said, and then I told her everything.

● ● ●

It was the first time in a very long time I heard the words about the car accident come out of my mouth. I didn't like to talk to anyone about that night. Not even Joss. And I hadn't had to. The whole of East Thumb was talking about it, and Joss had heard about the car crash from everyone else. But it was everything after the crash that had hurt the most.

The night of the accident was in November, two years ago. But sometimes it felt like it could have been yesterday. That night had been cold, like tonight. But it had smelled different. The air had an earthy smell to it, like a garden, after everything's been picked.

Mom was almost in her sixth month. After so many tries to have a baby and this time, everything was going so well.

Dad was driving. Mom sat next to him.

I was in the back seat behind my father.

The other car must not have seen us.

It smashed into Mom's side of the car.

Dad and I were okay.

Mom was not.

At the hospital, the doctor said he was very, very sorry. I didn't know right away it was because of the baby. Dad had to explain what the doctor meant.

Mom came home from the hospital a few days later. She lay in a ball. She didn't eat. She hardly spoke. And Dad had to pretend that everything would be okay.

"But it took a really long time," I said to Charlotte. I had stopped crying.

"I am so sorry, Lizzy. That is really awful."

"I realized the siren I had heard earlier that day must have been a warning."

"A warning?"

"A sign. But I didn't think about signs then. So I didn't know it was trying to warn us not to go out."

"You think that, really?" Charlotte's voice didn't sound like she thought I was weird. "I don't know anything about signs," she continued, "but I remember once thinking I should call my grandmother and the phone rang and it was her. My mom called it a coincidence."

"It could have been a sign," I said.

"The accident was not your fault—you know that, right? Even if that siren was a sign, how were you supposed to know that? And it wasn't even your idea to go see a movie."

"I don't think the accident was my fault," I said. "But now I look for signs that will give me a heads-up before stuff happens."

"How do you know when you see one?"

"I feel it here." I patted the place over my heart.

"What does it feel like?" Charlotte asked.

"It's like a little pinch. Like butterflies, except in your heart, not your stomach."

"It must be nice to know you can look for something out there," Charlotte said, waving her arm above her head, "that can warn you to brace yourself."

"Definitely," I said. "Don't you think life would be easier if you knew what was going to happen before it actually did? Like, take out all the surprises."

"Yeah. Maybe just the bad ones, though. Not the good ones. That's no fun," Charlotte said. "Plus, it sounds like a ton of hard work, trying to figure out what everything means. Isn't it tiring?"

I shrugged. I guess it did at times feel exhausting. But mostly it felt necessary. And safer. "I like having a heads-up for everything. Bad stuff so I can be prepared, and good stuff because if life stinks at the moment, it's nice to know I have something to look forward to."

"Maybe I should start looking for signs," Charlotte said.

"You should." I stared into the empty cup I was holding in my hands. "After the car accident, when my mom was really sad, I wanted to know if she would be okay. That's when I started looking."

"Where'd you look?"

"Sometimes the sky. Like, if the sunset was pink one day that meant Mom would be okay. Maybe not that very day, but eventually. Mostly I looked for signs in the puddle at the end of the alley. I'd leave the house for school and I'd say to myself, if the puddle at the bus stop is frozen, Mom will get happy again."

"Was it frozen?"

"It took a while."

"For it to be frozen? Or for your mom to get happy again?"

"Both," I said. "It didn't freeze until the middle of December. And Mom stayed sad until spring. But at least, according to the sign, I knew she'd be okay one day."

"You got to look forward to it?"

"Yeah."

Charlotte nodded. "Signs sound like hoping a little bit."

"I guess. Except you get to pick what you hope for. A sign, it just is what it is. Like you. You were a sign."

"*Me?*"

I reached forward and lifted her hand by her wrist. "I noticed this was a four-leaf clover the night I found you in my dad's truck. I knew it had to be a sign that you were good luck."

Charlotte tipped her head to the side like she hadn't heard me right.

"Are you mad?" I asked.

"Why would I be mad?"

"I don't want you to think that's the only reason I helped you."

"Why would I even think that? You helped me before you found me in the truck, right? You brought me food, and gave me your scarf." Charlotte turned her eyes away from me. "But I'm not good luck," she said. "Since you met me, a house burned down, your cat disappeared, and your dad had to go to the hospital."

"The house burned, but you didn't. My dad ended up being okay. I mean, my mom thought he was having a heart attack, and that wasn't the case. And Smoky . . . I was scared when he disappeared that he'd be lost in the school walls. But he's not. He found his way out."

"Uh-huh," Charlotte said. "But . . . this isn't a four-leaf clover. That's not what I drew. It's 4 Greenleaf Lane," she told me. "The address of the empty apartment. The building that burned." She pointed in the direction where the apartment house used to be. "I drew it on my hand when I ran away so I would remember where to find it. It wasn't ever meant to be an actual clover. Just four regular green leaves."

It wasn't a sign that she was good luck? I felt like I had swallowed a whole watermelon.

"Don't worry, Lizzy," Charlotte said. "If you think about it, it doesn't change anything, does it? Everything still happened the way that it happened. And it does look like a four-leaf clover, right? You can still think of it as that if you want to." Her words spilled out fast, like they were in a rush to make me feel better. I searched the trees for a branch bent in the shape of a smile, and then the dark sky for a cloud in the shape of something, anything to reassure me that it didn't matter Charlotte's clover wasn't what I had thought it was.

"I'm sorry if you thought I could bring you good luck. I . . ." She stopped suddenly. Her eyes stretched wide. Her mouth opened as if she had hollered, "OH!" which she hadn't. Then she said in a voice that was almost a whisper, "I'm sorry if you thought I could protect this baby."

Those words sounded so awful I wanted to cover up my ears. It was like I had rolled my sadness and scary stuff and all of my problems into a giant ball and handed it off to Charlotte. Handed? How about chucked? *Beamed?* Did I really believe it was up to her to make sure my mom had a healthy baby? All because of a four-leaf clover that wasn't even a four-leaf clover. The baby wasn't due for another six weeks. How could I have expected Charlotte to stay that long, anyway? Away from her own family. I felt my face burn. I couldn't look at her. I was such an idiot.

"I'm the one that should be sorry," I said. "I just wanted . . . I hoped . . ."

"It's okay to hope," she told me. "I do that a lot, too."

I nodded. I never realized it could hurt so much to breathe.

"Everything will be okay this time," Charlotte told me.

"You can't know for sure that it will," I said.

"You can't know for sure that it won't. But you can hope." And then she added, "So can I."

Charlotte reached across and grabbed my hand. I squeezed it. She squeezed back.

Then we sat squished together, our hands still connected, staring out at the twinkling sky without saying a word until I finally asked, "Have you ever heard of refraction?"

CHAPTER
23

"WHAT'S REFRACTION?" SHE ASKED ME.

I explained about the sun shining into the front room of the apartment house and its light bouncing off the glass mirror or one of the glass doorknobs and onto the leaves.

"Oh. That started the fire?"

"Yes."

"You knew this? When?" Charlotte asked. Her voice sounded calm, but her face looked like she was still processing everything I was telling her.

"I found out on Monday." She deserved to know the whole truth.

"Monday?" she said. Her voice sounded rougher. I waited for her to be mad. Worse than mad. Furious. Boiling. Raging. Never wanting-to-have-anything-to-do-with-me-ever-again angry.

Her eyes closed slightly, and she tapped her fingers against her thigh. She turned her hand toward me so I could see the faded green leaves above her thumb. She tipped her head slightly and said, "You didn't tell me because you thought I'd go home."

"I know you probably hate my guts right now. I should have told you when I found out the night Sergeant Blumstein was here." My heart was beating so fast I wondered if she could hear it. I didn't want her to hate me, but I didn't blame her if she did.

She shook her head. "I don't hate you at all."

"Why not?" I asked.

Charlotte pulled her head back slightly as if I had surprised her. "Because. I would have done the exact same thing," she said.

My mouth fell open. "What do you mean?"

"If I had found you in *my* dad's truck . . . if I thought *you* were good luck . . . if having you around could keep my dad from leaving me . . . *us.* . . . I wouldn't have told you about the fire, either. I would do anything . . . *anything* . . . to get my dad to stay."

And she pretty much had. Running away was drastic. But so was hiding a person in your closet and keeping the truth from them so they'd stay there.

We both sighed. "I don't know what do," Charlotte said. "When I thought I couldn't go home, I kind of wanted to. But I feel like as long as I'm away, my dad won't leave."

"It makes sense for you to go home," I said.

"Does it?" she asked.

"You left so your dad would stay, but you're gone. You're still apart." I waited for her to say something, but she didn't. "You still love your dad, don't you?" I asked.

Charlotte sniffed and wiped her nose. With the back of her hand, she wiped at her eyes. "Yes," she said.

"See," I said. "Just because someone leaves doesn't mean they stop loving you."

Maybe it was the fresh air or the great view of the moon or the awesomeness of being up on a rooftop. Maybe Charlotte suddenly remembered that her father still loved her more than the bajillion stars above us . . . because she nodded her head yes.

"I'm going home," she said.

"Okay," I told her. And I meant it.

• • •

By the time the bell rang and we were in our seats, there was a short stack of small red hearts on everyone's desk.

"What are these little hearts for?" Zoe asked, picking up her pile.

"We seem to be having some trouble filling up our board. I want to mention something important about what it means to 'Heart the World,'" Ms. Santorelli announced to the class.

"What?" Cooper asked.

She pointed to the big heart in the center of the poster

Charlotte had made for our Cozy Cat project. "Do you see how all these little hand-drawn hearts make up the one big heart? Well, *little* acts of kindness can add up and make a big impact, too, right?"

"I guess," Cooper said.

Ms. Santorelli walked over to his desk, wrote the word *help* on one of his paper hearts, and pinned it to the board. "I saw you help Zoe wipe up that mess in the cafeteria yesterday," she said. "Helping someone is 'hearting the world.'" *Kind of like what Bibi says about sticking your hand out when someone needs it*, I was thinking.

"I get it," Cooper said. "Good. Now I can quit trying to think of something big like a cat blanket or a port-a-potty."

"It's a port-a-*cycle*, jeez," Zoe said.

"Sorry. I meant port-a-cycle." Cooper wrote the word *apologize* on another heart and pinned it next to the one that said *help*.

Soon the little hearts filled in a lot of the empty space on the board.

Listen. Compliment. Smile. Share.

I sat at my desk tapping my pen while I thought about what to write.

Joss wrote the word *wash*. "I did the dishes last night, even though it was Elle's turn. She had a test to study for."

"That was nice of you," I told her. But I still couldn't think of anything to write on my heart. Until suddenly, the spaghetti in my brain wrapped itself around something totally obvious.

I thought about everything Charlotte and I had talked about last night on the roof. And the meaning of that heart-shaped puddle of spilled juice. It had been a sign. Not a sign of a defective heart . . . just one that wasn't quite right . . . one that had been broken.

I put my pen down and carried my paper heart, still blank, to the board.

"That heart doesn't *say* anything!" Cooper said as he watched me pin it up.

"Yes, it does," I told him. It said a lot. Like why Charlotte left her home to save her family. And why I hid her, and the truth, to save mine.

"It says *love*," I told him.

Ms. Santorelli had come up beside us. She saw the blank heart and smiled.

"That's something all of us can do to pay it forward," she said.

Then she wrapped her arms around me and squeezed with all her might.

• • •

I usually looked forward to Saturdays, but today Charlotte was leaving. I wasn't looking forward to that at all.

We had decided that with the crowd we would draw for our fund-raiser, and Franny's van blocking the view out the diner windows, it would be easy for Charlotte to slip away unnoticed.

Mom was at the diner with Dad, working today since Joss and I weren't.

Charlotte had changed back into her own clothes, which I had washed for her to wear home. I handed her twelve dollars for her bus ticket.

"I'm going to pay you back. I promise," she told me, stuffing the money in her pocket.

"Don't worry about it," I said. I pulled the directions to the bus station up on my phone and held the map up for Charlotte to see. "Just stay on Abbott all the way. It's a ten-minute walk."

"Thanks, but I know," she said. "I got here, remember?"

"Sorry. I'm nervous," I said.

"Me too," she told me. "It's going to be weird without my dad around. I probably won't get to see him much anymore."

"Remember what you said to me? That everything will be okay?" I asked.

"But I'm scared."

I grabbed both her hands. "You're the bravest person I know. You slept in an empty house and in a truck."

Charlotte shrugged. "I have a surprise for you," she said. "I was going to let you find it on your own, but I changed my mind." She ducked into my closet and sat down.

"What is it?" I asked, peeking inside.

"Come in here." She shifted over to make room for me, patting the floor beside her. The closet hardly had room for one of us, never mind us both. I squished myself into the small space next to her.

"I hope you like it," she said. Charlotte swept my hanging clothes out to the sides so they parted in the middle like curtains.

The first thing I saw were the colors from one side of the wall to the other. A bajillion of them. Like, every single color that ever existed. Then I saw me, giant compared to everything else she had drawn. I was stretched out on my side. I was pink-cheeked, and my face was a mix of blue and red, purple and brown. Reuben stood on my hip wearing a Cozy Cat sweater.

"I drew sweaters on the cats before you switched over to blankets," she explained. Fudge was there, too. He leaned against me, his face rubbing mine.

"Did you ever actually meet Reuben?" I asked her. Except for at night, Reuben spent most of his days under a bed or a chair.

"Not really," Charlotte said. "I saw him a couple of times when I went to use the bathroom. I knew it was him and not Fudge because he always bolted when he saw me. But of course I'd put him in the mural. I wouldn't leave any of your family members out."

"Awww," I said.

Behind me, Charlotte had drawn the diner. Above it was a pink sky and a smiling sun that looked like it was melting. Through the windows of the diner, people sat on stools at the counter. There were small plates of sunny-side up eggs, and their yolks were smiley faces, too. There was a stack of pancakes, glasses of OJ, itty-bitty forks and knives and napkins. I looked closer. On the pancakes, a little pad of butter was a melting sun that matched the one she had drawn in the sky.

I saw our rooftop porch, with a small bench, and two pots, filled with tomatoes hanging from bright green vines.

My mom stood on the top of the roof, cradling a baby. Standing beside her was my dad, in an apron so white it practically glowed. I hopped onto my knees and leaned in to touch it. Just white wall left untouched in the shape of the apron.

"How did you do that?" I whispered. Dad held a spatula above his head, like he was fist-pumping, *Yes! I made it to the top!* Waffles sat beside him, a dot of pink tongue hanging out of his mouth. I looked at my dog sound asleep on my bed. "Come see yourself," I said to him. But he kept on snoozing.

"Do you like it?" she asked me.

"Like it? I LOVE it!"

"Did you see Smoky?" Charlotte pointed to an outside corner of the diner that looked like a hole in the wall. Smoky was inside, next to a little TV and a small bowl of milk.

"He was watching TV all that time?" I asked.

"Who knows, right?" She laughed. "I'm there, too," she said.

"Where?"

"Not telling. You have to find me."

I looked where she had drawn my bedroom window, but I didn't see her.

"Where are you?"

"Keep looking," she said. "You found me before, you can find me again!"

My eyes wandered over and over the tiny drawings. A vase of flowers on a table, a napkin dispenser, the small OPEN FOR BUSINESS sign hanging in the window. I couldn't find her.

"Hey!" Joss called out.

I poked my head out of the closet. "In here!" I said. Smoky followed her into my room.

"Hey, Smokes," Charlotte said. "Hi, Joss."

Joss carried some Cozy Cat blankets, which she set down on the floor next to my desk. "What's going on in there?"

"Come see," I said. I scooted out of the closet so she could get a look.

"Wow! Charlotte, you did that?" Joss asked. "Can I have your autograph just in case we don't cross paths again before you become famous?"

"We are so going to cross paths," I said. "We're already trying to figure out a plan for how we'll pretend to meet for the first time."

"Make sure I'm there. I want to meet you for the first time, too," Joss said, her eyes still wandering over the mural. "Now, I have something for you," she said. She pulled Charlotte out of the closet and over to the mirror hanging above my dresser. "I looked through my stash of scarves for the one with the loosest stitches. You need good breathing holes because you're going to have to stay covered up for a while. We don't want you to suffocate."

"Well, thanks." Charlotte laughed.

Joss wrapped the scarf up Charlotte's face, stopping just below her eyes. I shoved a hat over her head and tucked in every last piece of her red hair. I handed her an old pair of Mom's sunglasses that I had in my desk drawer from Halloween.

"Why do you have to be so colorful?" I asked. Charlotte must have smiled when I said that. Her eyes turned into two sparkly green lines before she covered them up with the dark glasses.

"No one in a million trillion years is going to recognize me under all this," she said, staring into the mirror. "I wouldn't even know I was me."

"We have to go," Joss said. "It's nine thirty. We have to set up."

Charlotte lifted the sunglasses off her eyes and propped them on her head. She pulled me into a hug. "I'm going to miss you a lot," she said to me. "Thank you for everything."

"I'm going to miss having a roommate," I said.

"Don't forget about me!" Joss threw her arms around both of us.

"NEVER!" Charlotte and I shouted.

"And I won't ever forget you, either, Smoky." Charlotte broke away from our hug. "Look!" she said, pointing at the pile of Cozy Cat blankets. Smoky had curled up in a ball and was snoozing on top of the stack.

"How cute is that?" Joss said.

I took some pictures with my phone. "This is awesome publicity," I said.

Charlotte scooched down and kissed Smoky's head.

"So, Smoky is staying here?" Joss asked.

I explained how Charlotte and I had discussed Smoky last night because I wasn't positive if she had considered him her cat or mine. "You found him first," Charlotte had told me. "Plus, he's used to it here."

I thought that was really nice of Charlotte to say that. I wasn't entirely sure she was right about him being my cat first or not, but she was right that it was probably best for Smoky not to be uprooted again. That counted the most. Plus, there was the bus ride home to consider. Would he be allowed on? Would he need a ticket?

"Fudge and Waffles would miss him," Joss said.

"And Reuben?" I asked. We cracked up because Reuben wouldn't miss Smoky one bit, and we all knew it.

Joss and I gave Charlotte one last hug before we left. "Don't miss your bus," I told her.

"I won't," she said. "I'm leaving here at ten thirty." She pulled the blankets out of the closet and folded them up, laying the afghan across the bottom of my bed and the other on top of the books piled on my desk.

When I closed the door to the apartment and we booked it to the diner, my heart rolled into a tight, heavy ball. It stayed that way, taking up too much space for a while.

• • •

By ten o'clock, there was already a crowd in front of the diner. A table was set up on the sidewalk with free hot chocolate, coffee, and Bibi's awesome sticky buns. At the end of the table, far from the food and drinks, were the cat blankets and some shelter decals that we had fanned out.

The door of Franny's van was open, and a bunch of carriers full of cats and kittens were on display. Joss and I had put a cat blanket inside a few of them so everyone could see how perfect they were. The cats looked cozy curled up together on the knitted squares. A few kneaded their little paws into the soft stiches and purred. Franny had put a blanket over her shoulder and held one of the bigger cats up against it.

There was a long line for the blankets and one almost as long to see the cats.

"Look how precious," Ms. Santorelli said, peering into the van.

She was one of the first to arrive and had ordered two cat blankets—one for her sister's cat who lived way up north in the part of Maine everyone called the County, and a second one for her own cat in case the yellow sweater Joss had knit didn't work out.

"The cat blankets are a hit!" Joss's mom said. She was there with Elle. "Good for you, girls."

Mr. Sols poured himself a cup of hot chocolate. "I think we might need to take one of these beautiful cats home," his wife said to him, petting the one Franny was holding.

"Yes," Elle said to her. "Do it, they need homes."

Even though we were super busy, I kept looking over toward the alley for Charlotte. A half hour into our event, I glanced up just in time to see the back of her. I thought I saw her hand wave slightly, right before she turned out of sight.

I was surprised by the panic I felt filling up the back of my throat. I guess until right then I hadn't let myself think too much about what could happen when she finally went home. My brain was a knot of spaghetti. Charlotte promised she'd never tell where she'd been hiding, but what if she had no choice? What if those four green leaves *had* been lucky? And now what if, just like Charlotte, that luck was gone, too?

CHAPTER 24

JOSS RECOUNTED THE CAT BLANKET MONEY FOR the tenth time. "We have more than two hundred dollars already," she said as she stuffed the bills back in the money jar. "Some people are just giving us donations and don't even want a blanket."

"Score!" Cooper said to her. He shoved a sticky bun in his mouth.

"Hey. That's your third one," Joss told him.

He shrugged his shoulders and took another bite. "Is there a limit?"

"Yes. And you reached it two buns ago."

Mom poked her head outside. "Looks like all's well out here. You need anything?" she asked.

Maybe it was the way the sunlight hit her face, or it was because of the uneasiness I was feeling about Charlotte being gone, but Mom looked extra tired. She squinted at me. "How you doing on coffee and stuff?" She pushed the door open with her shoulder and waddled over. Mom carefully dumped a plateful of sticky buns onto the half-empty tray. "Here's the last of them," she said.

"Thanks," I said. "Are you okay?"

"Tired." She smiled and went back inside. I felt a pang of guilt. If it wasn't for the event, I'd be working right now instead of her. Maybe Joss should handle everything out here so I could take Mom's place and she could go upstairs and rest.

Pretty soon the free refreshments had run out and the crowd had dwindled to just a few people. All the cats and kittens were back in their carriers inside the van.

"Look here! We have six applications for adoptions!" Franny waved a fistful of papers at me.

Anyone who wanted to adopt had to apply first and be interviewed, kind of like they would apply for a job. Franny first made sure they would be good pet owners before she'd let an animal go.

"I am super proud of the two of you. Get over here." She pulled us into a hug.

As Franny smooshed the two of us up against the itchy plaid cape she was wearing, I was thinking there had been a lot of hugging going on today. Sad hugs when we said good-bye to Charlotte, and now happy hugs. I was feeling somewhere in between sad and happy . . . glad our event went well, but I couldn't stop thinking about Charlotte. Especially with her face staring at me all morning from the poster on the diner door.

Franny un-hugged us. "You two are dynamos! Now which one of you is going to head back to the shelter with me and help unload all these cats?"

"I will!" Joss announced.

"You can come, too, if you want," Franny said to me.

"I'm going to help out in the diner. My mom needs a break," I said.

After Franny and Joss left, I folded up the table and leaned it against the outside of the diner. I carried in the empty tray and thermoses. I saw Mr. Sols and his wife eating at one of the tables and waved.

"How'd it go?" Dad asked.

"Really, really good. We made almost three hundred dollars!"

"Anybody take home a cat?" Sid asked me. I told him about the possible adoptions.

"That's fantastic," Dad said. He was busy at the grill. "You going to help bus, now?"

"Yup." I dropped the stuff by the sink and washed my hands. "Where's Mom?" I asked, heading back out front to clear tables.

"Isn't she up by the register?" Dad ducked his head so he could see through the open space above the griddle. "There she is," he said. "You okay, honey?" She was sitting at the far end of the counter on a stool. "You go home. Lizzy's taking over now."

"Yes, okay." Mom smiled at him, but I could tell something wasn't right.

"What's wrong?" I asked, running to her. Bibi must have noticed because she came over, too.

"Stella," Bibi said, "you feeling all right?" But Mom didn't answer. She had her hands on her belly.

"Henry," Mom whispered. "Oh," she said, and moaned. Her eyes were glassy, and I saw a tear slide down her cheek. "The baby is coming."

"Mom!" I hollered. "DAD!" I screamed. My father looked up, and I heard the spatula clank when it hit the floor. Then Mom groaned. Her face was all distorted. "Oh," she said again. But this time it was much louder.

"Call 9-1-1!" my father yelled to Sid. He raced over to Mom and me. "All right, Stella, all right. It's all going to be all right," he kept repeating. He put his arm around her and brought his face close to hers.

Sid rushed over with a glass of ice water. "Here you go."

Mom shook her head no before she moaned again. I stuck my hand out for her to hold, but instead, she leaned forward and held her belly tighter. "It's coming. Now. Right now!"

People in the restaurant were staring. A couple of them had

smiles on their faces. Because they didn't know. They didn't know the baby wasn't supposed to be coming now. They didn't know that they weren't supposed to feel happy and excited. But most of the faces knew not to smile. The ones with panic in their eyes. The ones who knew us, and that this baby was coming six weeks too soon.

"No, no, no, no . . . ," my mother whispered. "No. It's not time." Mom looked at me. She was breathing heavily.

I heard a siren. It sounded far away, but in minutes it was right outside. The blue cruiser lights flashed inside the diner. The light turned Dad's face blue. Just like last time. Officer Hodge and Sergeant Blumstein burst through the door.

"The ambulance is almost here," Hodge told my father. "Don't you worry, Stella. We're going to make sure everything is all right." He saw that my mother was shivering. He took his jacket off and dropped it over her shoulders.

A bunch of customers jumped up. They helped Bibi and Sid pull tables and chairs out of the way to make room for the stretcher someone would be rolling in any second.

Mrs. Sols kneeled next to Mom. "Breathe, Stella, breathe," she said. "That's it, dear." Bibi pulled the elastic off her ponytail and tied back my mother's hair, which had fallen across her face.

Dad and Mr. Sols steadied her as she slid off the stool and brought herself to the floor. She was crying.

"MOM!" I screamed. Another siren was blaring. This time, I knew what it meant. This time, I knew what was coming. I felt my legs shake, and I grabbed the edge of the counter.

"Let them through," Dad told me when the EMTs arrived. Bibi moved me back and out of the way. "Help is here," Dad said to my mother. "It's all going to be okay." His voice cracked. I knew it had because he wasn't sure that it would be okay. How could it be? I didn't want to watch them wheel her away. I still hadn't forgotten the first time I had had to see that. So I did the only thing I could think of. I ran.

Out the diner, past the flashing ambulance, down the alley, I raced up the stairs to my room, and closed myself inside my closet. I squeezed my eyes shut and pressed my back against the wall. My heart pounded, and I took big gulps of air to stop myself from crying. I didn't want to make noise if anyone came looking for me. I didn't want to be found. I should have known this was coming. I should have begged Charlotte to stay.

I hopped to my knees and swiped my clothes to the side. I tapped the flashlight on my phone. Where had she drawn herself? I scanned the little hole where Smoky was hiding. I looked from one end of the wall to another. I double- and triple-checked the bedroom window. Where was she?

There! A teeny pair of hands gripped the sill. A few spikes of her red hair. Two slivers of emerald green peeking out between her fingers. I leaned in, shining my flashlight closer to the wall. I checked for the four-leaf clover tattoo above her tiny thumb. *You can still think of it as that if you want to*, she had told me. But it wasn't there. I wanted it to be. I wanted her to protect me. I wanted her to promise me that my mom would never leave me again the way she had after the accident.

My phone buzzed. A text from Dad.

In ambulance with Mom. Where'd you go? Find Bibi. She'll take you to the hospital. She's waiting in diner. Xxx

I wasn't going to the hospital. I was staying here.

I tried not to think about the last time Mom had gone in an ambulance. The last time I had been in a hospital was the night we had lost the baby. But that night, I had lost something else, too.

For months after the accident, Mom didn't care about anything anymore. Not the diner. Not Dad. Not me. I wanted it to stop. I wanted a sign that things would be all right . . . a promise that all the awfulness would go away. More than a pink sky or a frozen puddle, more than anything in the world, I had just wanted my mother.

I shined the light on my closet wall. My parents smiled at me. Charlotte had done a great job drawing Waffles and his one eye. As if on cue, I heard him bark and scratch at the closet door. I let him in and hugged him close to me. He licked the tears on my face.

The light from my room was enough to brighten the inside